The Promise of Time

Electa Jacobi

Contents

Chapter 1

Monday, May 19th 2003

Brisbane, Australia

2:03 P.M.

Today was Junie Bennett's tenth birthday.

She had a sour expression on her face as she trotted home from school with her hands tightly clutching the straps of her backpack. Junie cursed the day she was born. Two days ago during a tedious English lesson, Mrs David made the mistake of asking her what she thought about the pending event.

Truthfully, she'd told her birthdays were pointless. She was polite when she told the teacher that the purpose of a birthday was to celebrate the significance of a person. Although in her opinion, she continued, compared to the vast and endless universe in which they lived, people were insignificant. Therefore birthdays were futile. Birthdays only got a person closer to their death and death was certainly nothing to celebrate and neither was another ordinary day closer to it, cake or not.

Mrs David had commented on how dark Junie's outlook on life was for a nine-year-old and Junie had subsequently pointed out how naive Mrs David was for a forty-year-old woman. Junie was not surprised that this landed her an afterschool detention for two awfully boring hours.

School had dragged, the minutes had slowed, the hours had stretched for so long, she fear the day would never end. Mrs David knew very well how Junie felt about her birthdays. Even so, her teacher had still insisted on announcing to the class that it was Junie's birthday.

If that had not been aggravating enough, Mrs David had purposefully chosen the largest badge she could find and pinned it onto her shirt. IT'S MY BIRDTH-DAY, was printed in large, highly noticeable letters. She glared down at it. As much and as often as she'd tried – countless times throughout the day – Junie was not able to remove the badge.

It was in that moment that Junie came to the conclusion that she rather and intensely disliked Mrs David. She heaved a sigh and with a loud grunt, she kicked a nearby tin can. It rattled and clanked its way to the main road. She paused to watch as passing cars rode over it, repeatedly crushing and deforming the can until it was part of the road. Junie sullenly continued walking.

She wondered to herself, what had she been doing this time last year? Nothing important. That was her life, it seemed, she never did anything of any importance.

Junie heard the sobbing before she saw it. Up ahead, there was a small boy jumping and scurrying about as two other boys played with a bag, gleefully throwing it to each other.

It was Jake Ramsay and his weedy best friend Benja Pasternak. Every time she saw those two, they were either harassing some child or terrorising the neighbourhood. The smart thing to do, the coward's way, was to turn around and walk away. It wasn't any of her business. If she interfered, Jake and Benja would make sure her life was hell.

Yes, the smart thing to do, would be to turn around and walk away. Forget the boy. He was an idiot.

Junie did exactly that, she turned around and walked away, she had gone several steps before she stopped and grimaced.

But she was never one to do the smart thing.

Junie grasped at whatever scraps of courage she had left and channelled the anger she felt for Mrs David. She stomped back towards Benja and Jake. Junie had had enough of the two hooligans, they needed to be stopped and if nobody was going to do that, then she would have to.

"Hey!" she yelled, "Stop!"

Benja Pasternak turned at the sound of her irate voice. Unaware of the bag Jake had thrown back to him, it smacked him right in the face. He yelped and stumbling back, he fell onto the concrete floor. Benja swore as he pushed himself back up. He rubbed the side of his head where the bag had hit him. Jake glared at Junie.

"What is it pipsqueak?" Benja said, irritating painting his features.

"I'm not a pipsqueak!" Junie protested.

She really wasn't. She was tallest girl in her class. Benja and Jake may have been a year or two older than her, but she was the same height as them. Junie's eyes skipped to the small dark-haired boy, who was bent down with his hand on his knees, his breathing ragged and irregular as he coughed.

"Leave him alone," she said, not sounding as confident as she hoped.

Jake laughed and pointed to the large badge pinned onto her shirt, "is it your birthday?"

"No," she lied.

"Aw," Benja cooed, "you're ten years old today!"

The small boy was wheezing awfully loud now.

"I doubt your drug addict mum is even aware of what day it is let alone that's your birthday," Jake said. Benja laughed and they turned to high-five each other.

"Shut up!" Junie hissed, "she's not a drug addict!"

"No," Benja nodded seriously at her, "she's not just a drug addict but also a prostitute! The amount of men coming out of your house every hour is ridiculous."

Junie grit her teeth. Her eyes flickered to the small boy again, he was still coughing and his face had turned ashen.

Jake laughed, "Even my uncle had a go on your mum! We can't judge her of course, I mean, how else is she going to support her drug habit?"

Junie clenched her hands into tight fists to hide the fact they were now shaking. She could feel the tears prickling her eyes. She was not going to cry. She was not going to cry. Especially in front of these two.

"Happy birthday!" the two boys chorused and burst out laughing.

It was like a flash, a click, a snap. Something triggered right in her chest, and a rush of boiling wrath burst forth. Not pausing to think, or care, Junie lifted her foot and slammed it into Jake's crotch. He yelped and toppled to the floor. Quick as a flash, she did the same thing to Benja. He let out a girly screech. He dropped the rucksack as his hands flew to cup his groin and Junie took the opportunity to pick it up from the floor.

"Run!" she cried and grabbing the boy's hand, they dashed down the street.

Jake and Benja's shouts of indignation were not far behind as they chased after them. They crossed the road, the vehicles hooted noisily and several cars had narrowly missed running them over. Darting through the busy streets, Junie held onto the boy's hand as she took numerous twists and turns in hopes of confusing their pursuers.

If they were unlucky enough to be captured by the boys, Junie knew she could take a beating. She had done many times thanks to many of the neighbourhood kids but she doubted the wheezing boy could, he had probably never even been grounded, let alone experienced a punch. She couldn't protect him if he fell behind. Her heart was beating painfully hard in her chest. She pumped her legs faster, begging the dark-haired boy to keep running because if those two boys caught them, Junie couldn't guarantee that either of them would be able to walk again.

2:12 P.M.

Junie Bennett was lying on a grassy field, staring up at the clear afternoon sky, her chest rapidly heaving up and down as she tried to regain her breath. The dark-haired boy was kneeling beside her, panting just as hard. When she'd realised Jake and Benja had stopped chasing them, she'd stopped and collapsed onto the grassy floor of the extensive sports field. Junie sat up when she heard a string of aggressive coughs coming from the dark haired boy. His hand was clutching his chest tightly, the other covering his mouth.

"Oh my God," she stared at him, "What's wrong? Do you have asthma?"

He nodded. Junie leapt for his bag and frantically began searching through it. "Is your inhaler in here?"

He nodded again.

Junie panicked as she quickly scoured the contents of the rucksack. She grinned when she felt the plastic case of the inhaler. She passed it to the dark-haired boy and watched as he put it in his mouth. Several deep breaths later and the boy had stabilised. Junie stood up, she reached her hand out to him and the boy took it. He pulled himself up on wobbly legs and stretched his limbs. His short dark hair was now a sweaty mess, it clung to his forehead and stuck up at odd angles.

"Are you OK now?" Junie asked him.

"Yes," he croaked, "thank you."

It was the boy's eyes that caught her by surprise. The irises were coloured the most startling shade of blue. Blue like the Mediterranean oceans and the underwater landscapes of the pacific with striking flecks of sliver that reminded her of full moons. She must have been staring for too long because the boy gave her quizzical look. She quickly glanced away.

"No problem," she shrugged. Only it was a problem. It was a big problem. She couldn't walk down that street anymore. She would have to avoid Jake and Benja for several months at least, maybe for the rest of her life. "Don't worry about them, they're idiots."

Idiots that were likely planning how best to rip Junie apart. The blue-eyed boy looked about her age, although it was difficult to tell since he was so skinny and short. One corner of his mouth curved upward into a crooked smile.

"Dylan," the boy said, his voice still a little hoarse.

"What?"

"My name," the boy as he extended his hand, "I'm Dylan."

She stared at the hand for several seconds before grasping it and giving it a firm shake.

"Junie," she smiled, he had an odd accent, "you're not from around here are you?"

"I'm from New Zealand," he said, "I moved here about a week ago."

He opened his bag, and pulled out a clump of burgundy coloured rock. He showed it to Junie and her eyebrows furrowed in confusion as she wondered what he was doing.

"It's for you," he said, that crooked smile appearing again.

Junie hesitantly took it. She observed the rock with a cautious curiosity.

"It's a volcanic rock," he said, "it's from Mount Tongariro."

Junie looked at the boy, eying him suspiciously, "Why?"

"To say thanks for helping me," he answered with a nonchalant shrug, "you won't believe how many people just walked by."

She hummed thoughtfully, glancing back at the rock and rolling it around in her hand. This boy was rather odd. She looked at him and he looked right back at her, staring even, a kind smile on his lips and gratitude in his bright eyes. Very odd, she concluded. Junie smiled back, but normal had never been something she favoured.

The boy glanced down at his wristwatch – it was the Spiderman edition she'd been wanting for months now – and his eyes suddenly widened. He heaved the hefty rucksack back onto his shoulders.

"I need to go or my mum's gonna kill me," he said, and as he started jogging away, he glanced back at her, "Oh, and Junie?"

"Yeah?"

He grinned, "Happy birthday!"

He hopped over the low fence and zipped down the street, disappearing when he turned a corner. She stared at him, her eyebrows furrowing once more. How did he know it was her birthday?

"Oh," she mumbled, "the badge."

Junie glanced back at the rock. She smiled and shoved it into her pockets of her jeans.

2:32 P.M.

When Junie opened the door to her small dilapidated house, she—as usual—heard the sound of laughter mixed with an eighties song steadily playing in the living room. She took off her shoes and dropping her bag by the coat hanger, she crept forward. She paused near the living room door, where she could see her mother chatting with a man she didn't recognize. Junie frowned, her mother had brought along another one of her friends. Junie knew by now that it was best not to disturb her at times like this. She hopped up the creaky staircase and into her bedroom. As she eased onto her bed, she heaved a loud sigh.

Junie felt something dig into her thigh. She reached into her jean pocket and out the volcanic rock the boy – Dylan – had given her. Junie held it up into the golden bars of sunlight that streamed in through her bedroom window. As she observed it, quietly admiring its bur-gundy shade and the flecks that sparkled, Junie thought about the blue eyed boy from New Zealand. It was a sad thought really, that this small piece of volcanic rock was the first gift she had ever received.

"Birthdays suck," she muttered.

Chapter 2

Wednesday, May 19th 2004

Fortitude Valley, Brisbane

4:15 P.M.

Last week, Junie's school had announced that it was starting a class for gifted children. Students with the highest scores in the upcoming tests would qualify. There were twenty places in the class for each subject and Junie was determined to make into either Maths or Physics.

She knew she could it, because honestly, a good portion of the students at her school weren't too bright. Junie knew she could easily get in one of the gifted classes. All she had to do was study hard for the impending tests and she was in. Of course, that was easier said than done. She always had problems concentrating, especially a warm day like this. Junie flicked through her physics textbook, trying to find the page on electric currents. She sighed and wiped the sweat from her brow.

It was scorching hot in her bedroom, the air was humid and damp with the faint scent of cigarettes. Too much of the afternoon light had flooded in, it drowned her in its blistering heat, making it hard to focus on anything. She would pass out if this heat continued. Junie slid off her bed and started to stretch her arms and legs and once the feeling in her limbs returned, she yanked the curtains shut. It killed all the burning sunlight that had flooded the room.

She slumped back down onto her bed, and went back to reading the textbook. Now, electric currents --

"Junie!" Audrey shouted from downstairs, making her jump. "Junie!"

She sighed, closing her eyes for a few seconds before she answered. "Yeah?"

"Come down!" she ordered.

Junie slid off her bed and opened the door. She trudged down the creaky steps, wondering what Audrey could possibly want. In the kitchen, she found her mother leaning against the counter, a lit cigarette in her mouth and a glass filled to the brim with whisky in her hand. She pulled the cigarette from her mouth.

"Junie, my little darling," she said, blowing out a puff of smoke. "I need you to buy me a packet of cigs."

Junie fought an exasperated sigh. It was no secret that Audrey Bennett was an avid smoker and drinker. Junie would say her mother was an alcoholic but the last time she'd said that, she was given a look that meant she was five seconds from getting smacked if she didn't get out of her sight. She couldn't go a day without an alcoholic drink or her hourly dose of nicotine. If she didn't get it then she would snap and hiss at anyone who dared to come within three feet of her.

"Who's gonna sell me cigs? I'm underage," said Junie.

Audrey gave her a pointed look. She took a long gulp of the honey-coloured whiskey and let out a satisfied sigh. She said, "You know the charity shop next to the post office on Wickham Street?"

Junie nodded.

"There's a convenience store between the two," Audrey said, "just ask for a guy called Pete and tell him I sent you, he'll give you the cigs."

Junie frowned, "Audrey, I –"

Her mouth twisted into a scowl. "How many times do I have to tell you?" she snapped, "Stop calling me that. I'm your mum, so call me Mum."

Perhaps if she started acting like a mother, Junie might just consider it. Audrey pulled out a handful of cash from her purse and passed it to her daughter.

"There's eighty dollars," she said, sucking on her cigarette and letting out another cloud of smoke. "Buy three bottles of Lombard Whiskey, four packets of cigs, two packets of painkillers, and....a pack of apple ciders."

Junie glanced at the money, then back at her mother, "Can I buy some candy if there's change?"

"Knock yourself out," Audrey shrugged, "Go on then, what are you waiting for? Be quick, I have someone coming over in an hour."

Junie left the kitchen. She slipped on her dusty converses, and shrugging on her jacket she left the house. She skipped down the steps and hopped onto the cobbled ground. She paused, titling her head up to inspect the afternoon sky. The leaden clouds from this morning had floated away and left the sky a bright cerulean blue. Junie stuffed her hands into the pockets of her jacket and began her walk to Wickham Street.

"Junie!"

She turned around, expecting it to be her mother but was surprised to find it was the familiar blue-eyed boy running over to. When he finally caught up with her, he doubled over, breathing hard with his hands on knees.

"Dylan," she chided him, "why do you run when you know you've got asthma?"

"No...I..." He shook his head, "No....my... my..."

Dylan dug his hand into his jean pockets. He yanked out his inhaler and popped it into his mouth. She waited with an impassive expression as he sucked in long deep breaths.

"My...my asthma is getting better," he coughed.

Junie rolled her eyes. "Sure it is."

"It is," he insisted. He had to let out another a string of coughs before he could speak, "W-where are you going?"

"Gotta go buy something for my mum," she replied. She turned and continue her walk down the street, "You coming?"

Dylan nodded and despite the fact he'd almost had an asthma attack he proceeded to run after her. "Junie!"

"What is it New Zealand?"

Dylan frowned, "Don't call me that."

"What? New Zealand?" Junie grinned, "What? Don't you like being called New Zealand, New Zealand?"

His grimace confirmed his dislike for the nickname. Junie couldn't help but laugh.

It must have been a week or two after her tenth birthday, when Junie was called to the principal's office. She thought the school had figured out she was the one who had triggered the fire alarm – only because she had not studied for her physics test that day and there was no way in hell she was getting a C. Junie prepared her excuse, she had a whole speech planned out on why expelling her would reflect poorly on the school and how she would most definitely sue them if they did.

She was surprised upon entering the principal's office to find the blue-eyed boy she'd saved from Benja and Lucas sitting by the desk. The principal had assigned Junie the task of taking care of Dylan until he was used to life at the school. Apparently she was the best person for the job, which Junie thought was very poor judgment on his part. She had reluctantly agreed but it wasn't as if she had a choice on the matter. Junie had forgotten the boy's name and so she'd referred to him as New Zealand for a week.

He hadn't liked it and was very vocal about the fact. This only encouraged Junie to call him New Zealand more often. She liked the way his blue eyes narrowed and his mouth tightened each time. It would be endearing if it wasn't so funny.

It had been a year since and Dylan hadn't left her side. Somehow and somewhere along the line, she couldn't even begin to fathom why, Junie had grown quite attached to the blue-eyed boy from New Zealand.

"What are you doing for your birthday?" he asked.

Junie blinked. That was it. That was what had been nagging all day. It was her birthday. Her eleventh birthday. She glared at Dylan, mouth pressing into a frown.

Why did he have to remind her? She was having a perfectly pleasant day until he brought it up.

"Nothing," she answered.

"Nothing?" he repeated. He looked absolutely scandalised, "Why not? It's your birthday!"

Junie threw him a glare. "I don't care, New Zealand."

"But–"

"Just drop it." Junie snapped.

4:29 P.M.

Junie and Dylan paused outside the door of the convenience store, the stared up at the flashing neon sign that read Wickham Street Dailies. Dylan pushed the door and entered the store with Junie trailing behind. Inside, a waft of cool air washed over them, it carried the sweet scent of roses and fairy cakes. Junie glanced around the shop for a few seconds before marching towards to the counter. Dylan wandered off, probably because he'd spotted the comic book aisle. It was all he talked about these days, Iron Man this, Captain America that. It would be annoying if it wasn't so endearing.

The woman stood behind the counter was short and stout with unruly dark hair and a mole the size of Sydney Opera House.

"Uhm...is..."Junie began, trying to remember the name her mother had told her, "is...Pete here?"

The mole-woman swivelled round in her chair. "Pete!" she bellowed, startling Junie, "Pete! There's some kid here for you!"

Junie wanted to protest to that. She wasn't a kid. She was five foot two, the tallest girl in her year and she was eleven today. She heard heavy footsteps and caught sight of a chubby balding man walked through the door behind the counter.

"What?" the man called Pete asked grouchily. He looked like he had just been woken up from a rather enjoyable slumber.

The mole-woman nodded her head towards Junie, "This ankle-biter wants to see ya."

Pete's dark beady eyes instantly flew to Junie, "What is it?"

"Uhm...my mum wanted me to buy her some cigs and whiskey," she said.

Pete stared at her, his eyes narrowing. He suddenly grinned, revealing a row of blackened teeth. "You must be Audrey's little sprog. Bloody hell, you're the spitting image of her."

"Right," Junie drawled, "she wanted me to get three bottles of Lombard Whiskey, four packets of cigs, two packets of painkillers, and a pack of apple ciders!"

She felt quite proud of herself for remembering such an extensive list. God knows her mother would snap at her, if she missed just one item. In a less than a minute Pete had located the items and the mole-woman was shoving them into a plastic bag as Junie paid. She was sad to find there was no spare change. Junie sullenly turned to leave. She stopped, surprised to see Dylan standing before her and holding a basket full of junk food and comic books.

Junie's eyebrows furrowed. "Dylan," she said, "I'm not paying for that."

"Don't worry, you're not," he said, setting the basket on the counter. He pulled out some cash from the front pockets of his jeans and handed it to the mole-woman. Pete stuffed the items in a blue plastic bag and the mole-woman thanked Dylan for coming to the shop.

"Why did you buy all that stuff?" Junie asked as they left the store.

Dylan was grinning like he knew a secret. He tapped his nose and winked.

Junie rolled her eyes. This boy.

4:49 P.M.

Audrey wasn't in the kitchen when Junie and Dylan returned to her house. She pushed the door to the living room open. Her mother sat on the sofa with a lit ciga-rette in hand, as she chatted to a strange man beside her. They looked up when they heard the door creak.

"I've got what you wanted," Junie said. She scurried forward, pulling the items out from the plastic and setting them on the table.

"Thanks, love," her mother gave her a curt nod.

"This is your daughter?" the man with the scruffy beard and scruffier eyebrows asked. He stared at Junie, wearing an intense look of fascination that made her want to hide.

"Yeah," said Audrey, blowing clouds of smoke past her scarlet lips.

"She's pretty," he commented, his eyes scanned her lanky frame, "You're going to be very beautiful when you're older. Have you ever thought about modelling?"

Junie didn't like the way he was staring at her. He was practically leering, as if he was sizing her up. Junie shook her head, "Nah, not really my thing."

He cocked a bushy eyebrow, "Not really your thing? Y'know your mother was a model before she had you. The best in Queensland."

Audrey smiled and waved a hand dismissively in the air. "Oh, stop filling her head with stories," she smirked at him, "anyway, that was years ago."

"Stories?" the man grinned, "you were absolutely beautiful. You still are."

Audrey laughed in a way Junie had never heard, the sound reminded her of wind chimes in the summer air.

Audrey pulled the cigarette from her lips and stubbed it out on the coffee table. She smiled tightly at her daughter, "Junie, be a dear, get me and Craig some glass cups."

Junie more than eagerly left the room and walked into the kitchen, where Dylan was perched on the counter, munching on some of the potato chips he'd bought from the shop.

"Don't get any crumbs on the floor," Junie said as she reached up into the cupboard and grabbed two glass cups. She hated messy places. Her mother never bothered to clean and so the task was left to her. Junie went back into the living room, where Audrey was cackling at something the bearded man had said.

"Pour us some whiskey will you love," Audrey said and Junie did as she was told. She passed the drink to the man named Craig, and then one to her mother.

"Thanks," Craig said, still leering at her.

"Why don't you go play out for a bit?" Audrey suggested with another tight smile.

"I can't...I have homework to do." Junie said but as soon as she saw Audrey's warning glare, she nodded feebly and left the room once more. As she passed the kitchen, she called Dylan, "New Zealand, let's go!"

Dylan picked up his bag of goods and quickly followed her out.

5:26 P.M.

"It's so hot." Dylan whined.

"Yeah well," Junie sighed, "what're you gonna do?"

Junie and Dylan were sat by the Brisbane River. Junie had her feet immersed in the cool water. She had urged Dylan to do the same but the idiot was convinced there were flesh-eating creatures lurking in the river. Behind them, lay a dense forest, engraved with a long winding path that lead back to civilisation.

The stoic willow tree next Dylan, rained hundreds of its green tendrils down, shading the two friends from the pounding sunshine. Downstream, she noticed several sail boats and yachts drifting with the current. She briefly wondered what it was like to be rich and own a yacht as impressive as the one she saw. She wondered what it is was like, to live in a world where money was not a problem.

Junie breathed in the pungent smell of wildflowers and the salty scent of the river and smiled. She loved this place. She had discovered it two years ago on a detour from school. It had this serene essence that shrouded her with an odd yet welcoming sense of tranquillity. If she could, she would stay here for the rest of her days.

She glanced at Dylan. He was busy setting out all the things he had bought from the convenience store. There was an array of candy, potato chips, tea cakes, chocolate bars and two large bottles of coke.

Junie said, "Dylan."

He held up a rectangular pink box and grinned widely at her, "Here!"

"What is it?"

"It's your birthday present," he said eagerly, "just open it."

Junie took the box, she turned it around in her hand. When she saw the front she almost burst out laughing.

"Barbie?" she chuckled.

Dylan's wide grin faltered, "Don't you like it?"

"No," she laughed, "Why the hell would I want a Barbie doll?"

He shrugged, "I–I thought that's what all girls liked."

Junie sniggered, "Yeah, girls like Helen Torres but... I hate Barbie."

Perhaps hate was a strong word, she just never found any joy in play dress up with a plastic toy.

"Oh right..."he said. He glanced away, a tight frown pressed his lips together.

Junie sighed, feeling a spike of guilty strike her for hurting his feelings. She smiled softly at him. "But thank you for buying it, you're awesome."

The grin was back in a flash and it made her stomach knot.

Junie looked at the display he'd laid out. "What's this for?"

"For you," he said, "It's your birthday after all."

She pulled her eyebrows together. "I don't understand," she said, "Why did you do this?"

"Well...because you're my best friend," he said with a sheepish smile. "And, well, it's your birthday."

Junie blinked, not sure what to say. Most of the kids at school, either ignored or hated Junie because they thought she was stuck up. Something Junie found to be too funny to even take seriously. Were they blind? Could they not see her hand-me-down clothes? If they just took one look at her rundown house they would understand the last thing Junie Bennett was, was stuck up. Despite all the rude and untruthful things the other children said about her, Dylan still chose to hang out with her, which wasn't very good for his social status but he didn't seem to notice, let alone care. He was so odd she couldn't help but love him for it.

Junie stared at him. "Really?"

He nodded and Junie felt her smile grow into a bright grin because, well, because he was her best friend too. He slung an arm around her shoulder and pulled her against him. "Happy birthday Junie!"

Chapter 3

Thursday, May 19th 2005

Fortitude Valley, Brisbane

8:07 PM

Junie Bennett was three things.

She was cold, hungry and a little scared.

Cold, because for probably the umpteenth time that month the boiler had stopped working. She had tried to fix it herself with the boiler manual she'd found in the basement but she had, of course, failed miserably. The manual used such confusing vocabulary and complicated instructions that Junie had given up within fifteen minutes of her attempt. She wanted to call someone to fix it but the phone wasn't working and she didn't know who to call.

The temperature in the house had plummeted several degrees in the last ten minutes. The plus side was that she had been able to find something to keep her relatively warm. Junie wrapped the thick blanket around her and cuddled into its furry warmth.

She was hungry because the only thing she had to eat that day was an packet of crisps and an apple. Not even a nice apple at that. As soon as she had come home from school, Junie had ventured into the kitchen and just five futile minutes into her search for sustenance, she had found the cupboards and fridge empty with no food in sight. Well, there was that block of cheese but it had turned green. The food should have been here. Exhaustion and hunger never mixed well with her, it always seemed to make her irritable and impatient.

Junie was worried because she had not seen Audrey in four days . On the Monday morning before she had left for school, Audrey had trotted into the kitchen holding a suitcase. She was dressed to impress, her red hair had been styled upwards into a tight bun. She wore a short and rather tight white dress with crimson high heels. Audrey had given her some money for food and anything else she might need. She'd said she was going on a business trip with a friend of hers and that she would be back soon. Junie thought four days was soon enough.

She was, admittedly, a little scared because she didn't like the fact that she hadn't seen her mother for four days and she was starting to get worried. The lights weren't working again, leaving Junie to sit in the cold dark by herself. Junie may have been a little scared of the dark. The flickering light from the television ahead helped a little but not a lot. She sat in the living room, quietly watching an episode of Home and Away. She was only watching it because it was the only thing on television that she could tolerate.

Thump.

What was that? Her eyes scanned the room. She had definitely heard a noise.

Thump. Thump.

There it was again. Keeping the blanket wrapped around her, she sat up and cautiously left the comfort of the living room. The narrow hallway was dark. The thumping noise was coming from the front door. Junie frowned. Who would be knocking at this time? For a second she thought her mother had returned, she shook her head, batting the thought away when she realised her mother would have come in from the back door.

Thump! Thump! Thump!

Whoever was knocking was getting impatient now. Junie hopped forward and grabbing a baseball bat from the storage compartment underneath the stairs, she walked towards the door. If she was going to die, she was going to die fighting.

Thump! Thump! Thump! Thump!

She raised the bat high and yanked the door open. She was surprised to find that on the other side of the door was not the bloodthirsty monster she expected but the skinny blue-eyed boy by the name of Dylan Mercer. He gaped at her. His ocean blue eyes were widened in fright. Junie dropped the bat and let out an exasperated sigh.

"New Zealand," she huffed, "You bloody idiot."

"Were you about to hit me with that baseball bat?" He asked and she nodded, "Why?"

"I live in Fortitude Valley, in case you haven't noticed." She snapped, stepping aside to let him in. She shut the door, and locked it securely behind her. "It isn't exactly a safe place."

"Why's it so dark?" He asked glancing around.

"Light's not working," she said. In the dim light she noticed that he was holding a large bag. "What are you doing here?"

"I'm here to celebrate your birthday, you divvy."

Junie rolled her eyes. She was hoping he'd forgotten. "Do your parents know you're here?"

Dylan nodded, "My mum dropped me off just now. She said I could sleep here tonight."

"Uh...I didn't say you could sleep here tonight."

He shrugged, "Don't care, I'm staying. I don't like you spending your birthday alone."

She was suddenly thankful for the dark because he couldn't see the crimson red blush that was painting her cheeks.

"Idiot," she mumbled.

"Good thing, I brought some light," he grinned and flicked on a bulky torch he held. It lit up the hallway, casting everything in an eerie glow. He passed it to her and began rummaging through the bag. "I know how you love chocolate cake...so I thought it would be cool if we made some!"

She smiled. "Okay."

Dylan grinned again, revealing the silver braces he had gotten a few months ago.

8:19 P.M

Junie had located several lamps from around the house and dotted them throughout the kitchen. They needed a copious amount of light if they wanted to make the chocolate cake. She was thankful the oven and all the other items in the kitchen were working perfectly.

Junie pulled her red hair up into a messy ponytail. She picked up the bag of flour and she poured the contents into a bowl as Dylan chucked a handful of spices and bicarbonate soda. He dumped a chunk of butter into the bowl and began mixing and kneading it with his fingers.

"Is your mum still away?" He said.

"Uh-huh."

"Four days now..." he frowned, "Where d'ya think she is?"

Junie shrugged, "She said somethin' about meeting a friend."

"My mum would never leave me alone in the house for so long," he said. Junie threw him a glare and he quickly apologised, "I'm sorry, I didn't mean..."

"It's alright," she said as she poured sugar, treacle, syrup and milk into the saucepan. She turned on the stove and let it cook for a few minutes.

Junie didn't want or like to admit it but he was right.

His mother would never do leave him like that. His mother was a kind woman, she always smiled and always made them pancakes every time Junie visited. Unlike Audrey, she didn't smoke, she didn't drink and she certainly didn't treat Junie like her own personal slave.

She loved his father, he thought she was a bright girl, he had introduced her to some of the most fascinating books on astronomy. His two older sisters were kind too and Bethany always knew how to make her laugh. Dylan came from a privileged background. His father was the Chief of Medicine at Brisbane Private Hospital and his mother was a successful romance writer. She had seen Audrey and some of her teachers reading his mother's books. Although when Junie had tried to read some of the books Audrey had admonished her and said the books were strictly for grown ups.

Junie regularly went to Dylan's house and some days she would sleepover. The only word to describe his house was magnificent. It was a magnificent mansion, luxurious and warm and so homely. Dylan's family was rich. He could have everything and anything he wanted at just a snap of his fingers.

She glanced at him, watching as he stirred the bowl of flour and egged. She was puzzled as to why he was friends with her. He could be friends with people much better than her, so why her? She didn't have much to offer him.

9:22 PM

"Wait, wait, wait, wait," Dylan said. He searched through his bag once more and pulled out a small plastic packet. He counted to himself as he plopped the small candles into the cake, "nine...ten...eleven...and because you're twelve today...we add one more...twelve!"

They had finished making the chocolate cake was finished and in all honesty, it looked absolutely delicious. Dylan had successfully made the lemon icing and dribbled it on top of the cake. They moved all the lamps from the kitchen and into the living room. Dylan ignited a match and carefully lit all the candles.

He glanced at Junie with a broad grin, "Make a wish!"

She returned his grin. For the first time in her life, Junie had a birthday cake. A delicious looking birthday cake. She pondered for a few seconds, contemplating her wish. Dylan and Junie were half way through the school year and even though she hadn't made any new friends (apparently she was too rude and didn't know when to shut up) but she didn't care because she had Dylan.

Junie leant forward and closing her eyes she made her wish.

I wish Dylan and I will always be together.

She puffed out her cheeks and blew. The fire on the candles flickered for a second before they died, and wisps of smokes drifted slowly up from the tips.

"Woo-hoo!" Dylan cheered, "And now to cut the cake."

He took a sharp knife in hand and began slicing the chocolate cake into quarters. He placed a slice of the cake on Junie's plate and one on his.

"Happy birthday, Junie," he said.

She grinned, "Thanks New Zealand."

Chapter 4

F riday, May 19th 2006

Fortitude Valley, Brisbane

3:29 PM

The sun sat perched at its highest point in the sky and its heat beat down on her bare shoulders as she walked home. Her hair, brighter than the sunshine and the vivid colour of burning fire, had escaped from its ponytail and was now flowing down her back in red waves.

Her breaths came fast and heavy and her heart was still hammering in her chest. She had been running for almost twenty minutes from a pack of dogs and she would be lying if she said she wasn't exhausted. She didn't know why she kept taking that shortcut. It just wasn't worth it with those dogs lying in wait.

The first thing Junie noticed, upon entering her house and shutting the door behind her, was the abnormal silence. Her house was never silent, silence was a stranger. It was always filled with either Audrey's loud cackling laughter, an eighties song blaring away or the incessant voices of Audrey arguing with another one of her male companions.

"Audrey?" She said tentatively stepping further into the hallway. "Audrey, Audrey are you there?"

Junie called her mother's name several times but the irritated quip she always gave in answer never came. She wasn't in the kitchen, living room or the back yard, and so she proceeded to look upstairs. She wasn't in her bedroom or Junie's.

Junie walked down the corridor and pushed open the door to the bathroom. She froze. Her brown eyes widened and fixed on her mother's motionless form. She was lying on the marble floor, passed out and surrounded by dozens of bottles whiskey and vodka. For the first few seconds all Junie did was stare before she snapped out of stupor and rushed to her mother.

"Mum!" She gasped she dropped to her knees beside her. Panic clawed at her as she shook Audrey by the shoulders and patted her cheek. She almost cried in relief when she saw her mother's eyelids slowly flutter open.

Audrey let out a groan.

"Oh my God," Junie breathed, "Mum, what have I told you about drinking so much?"

Audrey brushed strands of red hair from her eyes and groaned once more. She blinked dazedly up at Junie and a grimace formed on her lips. She batted away Junie's offer of help and lazily pushed herself up into a sitting position.

Her fingers rubbed her temple in slow circles, "I have a blinding headache."

"What were you doing?" Junie asked.

Audrey glanced at her daughter and gave her a weak smile that only increased Junie's worries. "Nothing, just...got a bit carried away, I'm fine, love."

Audrey looked like the definition of awful. Dark circles painted her tired and bloodshot eyes. Junie noted that she had been wearing those grey sweatpants and tank top for three days now. After a few moments, Audrey stood up and walked over to the cupboard.

She pulled out a bottle of vodka and a packet of cigarettes before she promptly left the bathroom, leaving Junie to sit on the cold marble floor and process what had just occurred. She gulped and closed her eyes for a few seconds.

She couldn't stay here, she couldn't stay here as her mother drunk herself to death. Junie left the bathroom and entered her room. She found a spare scrunchy and pulled her back into its usual ponytail. Grabbing her skateboard, Junie hopped out of her house and headed to Dylan's house.

4:11 PM

Junie pressed the doorbell and hoped he was in. Last time he had been at his grandmother's and she'd had to spend the three hours in the library in order to avoid going home. She could faintly hear the sound resonating throughout the house. She had not just travelled thirty-minutes on her skateboard in the sweltering heat for the fun of it.

When no answer came, Junie pressed the doorbell once more and sighing she glanced up at the cloudless sky. The door swung open and Junie's head snapped forward to see one of Dylan's older sisters stood before her. She was soaking wet and dressed in a floral pink bikini. Her long dark hair was drenched with water, causing it to stick to her shoulders and back.

Junie smiled, "Hi, Lena."

Pulling the lollipop out of her mouth with a short popping sound, Lena Mercer gave her a tight smile that disappeared as fast as it had appeared. She asked, "You want Dylan right?"

"Yes, is he in?"

Lena nodded. She opened the door wider and stepped aside. Junie quickly strode into the hallway of the house as Lena shut the door. She walked past her and staring up, she paused at the bottom of the staircase.

"Dylan!" Lena suddenly bellowed, her shrill voice made Junie jolt in surprised, "Get your arse downstairs! Your mate's here to see you!"

It was only a few seconds later that the New Zealand native came bounding down the stairs. He skipped the last step and landed on the dark brown floorboards with a loud thud. Dylan glanced at his sister, frowning slightly, "Mum's gonna kill you, she said no swimming in the pool and you brought your boyfriend over again."

"Bite me," Lena snapped before turning around and sauntering into one of the many rooms in the hallway. Dylan's ocean coloured eyes found Junie's and an elated grin spread across his features.

"Happy birthday!" He shouted and threw his hands in the air, "You're thirteen today! Finally a teenager!"

"Don't remind me," Junie grumbled as she dropped her skateboard by the coat hanger.

She was surprised when he suddenly rushed forward and grabbed a hold of her hand. He started pulling her up the staircase and grinned at her, "Come on, I've got this new game, its epic."

She didn't know whether it was by accident or whether he did it on purpose but when he lightly squeezed her hand, licks of fire danced joyously in her stomach. His hand was warm and soft in hers.

She swallowed as she stared down at their joined hands and managed a shaky nod. "Okay."

Dylan and Junie reached his bedroom, she ignored the warm tingling sensation that lingered when he let go of her hand. Dylan shut the door and scurrying forward, he eagerly pointed to a large television that was mounted on the wall.

"Mum bought me a TV!" Dylan announced, his arms flying up in gleefully.

Junie stared at the plasma screen television, awed and astounded. She gasped, "But your thirteenth birthday was two months ago."

"Mum said if I got an A in my Geography exam, then she would buy me it," he beamed, "And look...she got me this as well."

Junie's eyes widened at the sight of the video game he was holding. "Hitman: Blood Money?" She spat, "But...t hat's not even out yet!"

"Dad's friends with the guy who created the game, so she got him to pull some strings," he grinned, "You wanna play?"

"Hell yes!" She said nodding eagerly.

As soon as Dylan switched on the PS2, the two friends began playing. Dylan really should not have been surprised to find that he was losing spectacularly to Junie.

It had become the norm. He always lost every time they competed in these video games.

"Yes!" Junie cried. She had won yet another match. "Suck on that!"

Dylan huffed, "that was a fluke."

"Yeah," she replied with a scoff, "so were the other twenty times."

His eyes narrowed, "Rematch."

"Fine," Junie smirked as she settled back into the bean bag, "Prepare to get your arse kicked yet again, New Zealand."

8:05 PM

"Come here!" Junie shouted.

Dylan laughed as she chased after him. On their tenth rematch Dylan had shamefully resorted to kicking the control pad out of her grasp and subsequently caused Junie's player to be killed in the most gruesome manner. He had noticed the irritation and shock burning in her chocolate brown eyes and immediately started running. And for the past ten minutes Junie had been running after him. He was going to pay.

Dylan's twin sisters , Lena and Bethany were irritated beyond belief when the two friends came blundering through the living room and into the back garden. Junie leapt forward and reaching out, she grabbed Dylan by his shirt. They stumbled and both fell to the grassy ground. Junie instantly rolled on top of him and strad-dling his waist, she ruffled his dark hair and punched his arm.

8:23 PM

In the back garden, Junie and Dylan lay on the grass and stared up at the black sky. The evening air spun light and cool between them; it carried the comforting scent of lavenders and roses.

"Junie." Dylan said.

"Mm?"She hummed in response.

"What do you want to be when you're older?"

"An astronaut maybe," she answered and shrugged, "Something to do with space."

Dylan glanced at her as she looked up at the sky. She could hear the amusement in his tone as he said, "An astronaut?"

"I know it's bit farfetched but..." she paused, daydream-ing for a second about being on a space station and staring down at the earth, "I would love to float like eighty thousand miles above the earth, it sounds crazy but...it seems like an easy life for me."

Dylan chuckled, "You're crazy."

"Aren't most astronauts?" She said, "What about you? What do you wanna do?"

"I want to work in music," he replied, "I'm getting bet-ter at the guitar and piano."

"I can imagine it now..." Junie turned to look at him, surprised to find that he was already looking at her. His blue, blue eyes locked on hers. When he was so close, her thoughts were scattered, jumbled things. "Um....ten years....ten years down the line, you'll be standing in a sold out concert dressed in leather and platform boots, rocking your guitar to one of your songs."

Dylan laughed and she didn't realise how lovely of sound it was until then. He crinkled his nose, "Not sure about the platform boots...but I like the leather."

"You're an idiot. All the legends of music wear platform boots."

"Hey!" He said, "Respect your elders."

"Please," she rolled her eyes, "You're only two months older than me."

"I'm still older," he countered.

They stared at each other for a moment the only sound coming from the chirping crickets and the tweeting birds.

"D'ya miss New Zealand?" She asked softly.

He shrugged, "Not really, I love Australia. It's not like I have anything to miss back in New Z. To be honest, I didn't have any friends."

"You didn't?"

He licked his lips and his blue eyes flitted away from her and up at the blackened sky, "No, you were my first friend."

Junie felt something twist in her chest and she suddenly had the urge to hug him and never let go. Dylan sat up and started rummaging through the pockets of jeans and pulled out some sort of jewellery piece. She sat up, so she could see what he had in the palm of his hand. It was a bracelet. A pretty bracelet that was made up of colourful little beads that spelt out her name.

"Here," he said grasping her hand and slipping it onto her wrist. He looked at her, smiling so heartwarmingly shy, "I made it myself, well, Bethany helped me since she's good at making stuff. Do...do you like it?"

Junie felt rather dazed for a long moment, her heart rate speeding up as she turned the bracelet around her wrist. She swallowed. The bracelet was so beautiful in its simplicity. The fact that it had her name on it added volumes to the brilliance of the gift.

"Junie?" He said looking at her with a worried expression.

Dylan was staring at her with big blue eyes. Sometimes, she thought they were just too blue to be real. Nobody's eyes could be so bright. It just was not possible and yet he was the proof that it was.

Things had been different lately. She wasn't sure whether it was good different or bad different, she just knew things were different. For example, in the past few months or so, Junie had been seeing Dylan in a different light. Lately, Junie couldn't stop noticing how exceptionally cute her best friend was.

The warm laugh, the goofy grin, the electric blue eyes, those were just a few things that she had began to adore about him. A few weeks ago during an English lesson, Junie had found herself gazing at Dylan for an abnormally long time and in that moment Junie had realised something. Somehow and somewhere along the line, Dylan had shifted from just Dylan to Dylan, Dylan, Dylan, Dylan times a million. Somehow and somewhere along this painful line they could life, Dylan could make her heart sing and transform hell into heaven and heaven into hell.

"Junie," Dylan said, yanking her back to reality.

She blinked, "Uh...sorry what?"

"Do you like it the bracelet?" He repeated

She nodded, "Yeah, God, yeah. It's brilliant! Thanks, New Zealand."

And he grinned in that way that made her heart jump in her chest, "Happy birthday Junie."

Days, weeks and months of denial all washed up in this moment. Juniper Theresa Bennett had a crush on Dylan

Samuel Mercer. It was official, with middle names and everything.

Chapter 5

Saturday, May 19th 2007

New Farm, Brisbane

1:31 PM

"So, what did the doctor say?" she asked.

Her mother pulled a pair of sunglasses from her inner jacket pocket and put them on. She shrugged, "The baby's fine."

"No..."Junie said, "The gender, what's the baby's gender?"

"Boy," her mother answered tersely.

Junie smiled. A little brother, she was going to have a little brother.

She was tempted to ask who the father was but knew it would be a fruitless endeavour. Very much like each time she asked Audrey who her father was. She never received a truthful or straightforward answered, just a sharp scolding for apparently talking about irrelevant matters.

It was in October of last year that Junie had found out about Audrey's pregnancy. She had been scouring the living room for the Geography textbook she had misplaced when she had saw a white plastic stick poking out of the bin.

A white plastic stick that she had immediately recognised as a home pregnancy kit. And it had been positive. Junie spent a good hour panicking about it, so much so that she had grabbed her skateboard and rushed over to Dylan's house. Who, by the way, was not at helpful in calming her down. It was two weeks later that Junie finally dredged up the courage to ask her mother about the pregnancy.

Audrey had shrugged and said, she wasn't sure whether she wanted to keep the baby. At first Junie wasn't either. In all honesty, a baby was a big deal and considering how low on money they were, how Audrey had been fired from her job and how she was already struggling to pay the bills, Junie just couldn't see how they would cope with another mouth to feed.

But one day, Junie had caught sight of her mother's pregnancy bump and she realised something. She realised that that bump was her future sibling. That bump was her future brother or sister. And that thought, that realisation, almost made her cry because she knew she would never forgive herself, if she let her mother give the baby up for adoption. The baby needed to stay with its family not some strangers. Yes, the Bennett's were not the strongest or the most traditional of families but they were still family and that's what mattered.

"Right, I'm going to see one of my friends," Audrey said, "I'll see you later."

Junie shook her head, "Don't drink any alcohol or smoke."

"I haven't drunk or smoked since I found out I was pregnant have I?"

It was true but that was probably because the doctor was keeping an alarmingly close eye on her and she was being forced to go to weekly pregnancy sessions at the clinic. Which, Junie, liked to accompany her to, just to make sure she actually went there.

"Don't worry, we're only watching some movies." Audrey said.

Junie nodded but she still wasn't convinced.

3:20 PM

Bobbing her head to the Arctic Monkeys track blasting in her earphones, Junie steadily rode her skateboard down the street. She grabbed a tightly rolled up newspaper from her bag and momentarily pausing, she threw it ahead. It fell onto the doorstep of a brightly coloured bungalow

She only had ten more houses to visit and then she could go back to Wickham Street Dailies and get her thirty dollars pay. Junie felt rather neutral about delivering newspapers. The pay wasn't great but it wasn't bad either. It was a job. It gave something to do and they really needed all the money they could get for the baby.

Junie frowned. She realised that she needed to take the shortcut if she wanted to finish early so she could go to Dylan's. She liked his house, she loved being with him. He made her forget all the troubles she was having at home, he made her feel like she was still a child, not somebody who needed to chip in for the household bills if they didn't want the electricity to be cut off again.

Junie hated taken the shortcut, if wasn't for rabid and bloodthirsty dogs she would have quite enjoyed it. But these dogs loved to chase and torment her every time. She turned a corner and cautiously began walking down the narrow and sunless path.

Maybe you'll be lucky this time and they won't even be there.

As soon as that thought came to mind, Junie saw them and as soon she saw the dogs, Junie picked up her skateboard and ran for her life. The usual hunger for her flesh was evident in those dark beady eyes. She spotted the fence overhead and pumped her spindly legs forward. She chucked her skateboard over and with a grunt quickly hopped over it herself. Junie collapsed and crashed onto the patch of dandelions. She ignored the sharp pain in her knee and pushing herself up, she scrambled away from the fence.

The dogs couldn't get past the fence and she thanked the heavens or whoever was sitting on a cloud up there. They bared their teeth as they growled and snarled viciously at her. Feeling rather triumphant, Junie stuck out her tongue and laughed.

With one last glance at the dogs, she picked up her skateboard and stepped out onto to the street lined with bungalows.

Junie finished ten minutes earlier than she had expected. It took her a few seconds to realise she was on the highest point of the hilly street. Below the road was lined with vehicles, it was steep with thrilling sharp twists and turns. Junie grinned, she positioned the skateboard in the middle of the road and hopping on, she pushed herself forward.

The cool wind whipped her flaming hair back as the skateboard sped down the steep hill. She easily tackled the abrupt turns of the road, she bobbed and weaved past several pedestrians and even managed to perform the new trick she had learnt. Junie finally came to a slow stop at the bottom of the hill. Her heart was racing and she grinned from the thrill of such an intense ride. She glanced up at the hill, laughed and decided to do it again.

3:59 PM

Bethany Mercer opened the door for her. She smiled and stepped aside. Junie eagerly entered the house. In comparison, Bethany was a lot kinder than her older twin. Lena was easily riled, she had a short temper and ninety percent of the time she was sarcastic. Bethany did have her sarcastic moments but she was easier to talk to, more relaxed.

"Dylan's in the kitchen," she said.

"Thanks," Junie smiled return. She dropped her skateboard in its usual place by the door and walking down the hallway, she opened the second door to the right.

As she expected, Dylan was sat on one of the stools that surrounded the island counter, lazily munching on a sandwich.

"Hey, New Zealand," Junie said.

He looked up at the sound of his nickname and grinned widely at her, "Oh hey, Junebug."

Junie's stomach twisted in a thousand knots at the sight of his grin. "Stop me calling me that," she frowned.

"Stop calling me New Zealand." He said.

Dylan glanced at his plate of sandwiches and flashed another smile, "Want a sandwich?"

"What it's in it?"

"Chicken, bacon and mayonnaise," he answered, "I made it myself."

Junie picked up a sandwich and tentatively bit into it. Dylan's cooking was always disastrous, so you had to forgive her if she expected it to taste like dead horse. However, she was pleasantly surprised to find it didn't taste like a dead horse but rather...pleasant.

Junie smiled. "It's pretty good, Dyl."

Dylan walked over to the fridge, he opened the door and glanced back at Junie, "Want drink do you want?"

"Orange," she answered as she took another bite of the sandwich.

He bent down and pulled out a carton of the juice. Shutting the fridge door, he took a glass cup from the cupboard before placing the carton and cup on the counter.

"Here," he said, pouring the orange juice into the glass cup and passing it over to her.

She smiled and she took a sip of it, "Thanks, New Zealand."

"So," he began, "It's your fourteenth, you excited?"

Junie snorted, "Why would I-?"

She was cut off by the sound of someone singing-ice. She looked up to find none other than Helen Torres sauntering into the kitchen. Confusion flashed on Junie's face for a moment before her features quickly contorted into a mask of disdain for the olive-skinned girl.Helen slipped onto the stool beside Dylan.

"Junie," Helen said in a sickeningly sweet tone with that sickeningly sweet smile- that was so obviously fake - plastered on her face.

"Helen," Junie said through gritted teeth. She threw a confused look to Dylan, who just glanced away, looking sheepish and rather guilty.

"I like your top," Helen said, "My grandma has one like that."

Junie's eyes skipped back to her, glaring hotly, "Well, even your grandma must have better taste you then."

Helen's syrupy smile faltered, "Go to hell."

"As long you're not there."

"You should do some soul searching," Hellen suggested, that sickeningly sweet smile back, "Who knows, you might just find one."

Dylan glanced back between the two, watching nervously as the heated conversation grew. Junie opened her mouth to shout a flurry of obscene and unflattering insults at the dark-haired girl but was interrupted by Dylan quickly saying, "Hey, Junie, can I talk to you for a sec?"

Before Junie could decline or even do anything, Dylan sprang up from his seat and grabbing her hand, he pulled out of her kitchen. He led her down the hallway and into the living room. Once he shut the door, he whipped round to face his best friend who had her arms folded across her chest and gave him a fierce stare.

"What the hell is that she-devil doing here?" Junie demanded.

"I told her she could come over because she said wanted some help on her science homework."

"But you're not good at science and neither she is," Junie quirked an eyebrow, "so, why would you wanna help her?"

Dylan's eyes fell to the floor as he nervously shuffled on his shoes on the carpeted and Junie felt her heart drop into her stomach.

"Wait, do you like her?"

The crimson blush that dusted his cheeks was the answer.

"What?" she swallowed the lump forming in her throat," "Why?"

Dylan shrugged, "I don't know...she's cute...and I think she likes me too."

Junie balled her hands up into tight fists to hide the fact that they were now shaking. Stupid Dylan. Really, really stupid Dylan. What was he doing liking someone as shallow, self-absorbed and bitter as Helen Torres? But the answers were clear as day. Because she was Helen

Torres. Popular and beautiful and charming. Every boy in their year had fallen under her spell.

Junie shook her head, "You can't like her."

He looked at her then, eyebrows furrowed in that utterly adorable manner. "Why?"

Because he should have liked her, not Helen. Helen didn't know him like she did. God, but Junie couldn't compete with someone like Helen Torres. Helen was petite, beautiful with her olive-skin and hazel eyes. Junie sometimes felt she was too tall for thirteen - no, fourteen now. Five foot five and still growing. She had a feeling she would end up like her mother, too tall and too graceless to be saved.

"Because," she mumbled. You have me. "Just....because, okay?"

Dylan wasn't too convinced with her answer. He sighed and said, "Well, she's leaving in ten minutes anyway. Once she's gone, we can go skateboarding."

"Hm." She said as she absentmindedly fiddled with the bracelet he had given her for her birthday last year.

"You know," he began in a teasing tone, "I ordered your birthday present but it hasn't come yet."

Junie looked up at him, a smile threatening to form on her lips. "What is it?"

"That would be telling," he chuckled and lightly bobbed her nose, "Since I don't have your present right now, I am going to give you a hug!"

In that instant Dylan wrapped his arms around her. He pulled her against him and enveloped her in a warm hug. She was surprised at how quickly she relaxed into him. Her eyes closed and a content smile pulled at her lips as she dropped her chin onto his shoulder.

"Happy birthday Junie," he whispered softly in her ear, his warm voice sending shivers down her spine.

She hugged him back, perhaps a little too tightly but with Helen Torres in the next room, waiting to whisk Dylan away, she couldn't help it. She could feel his heart softly beating against her chest.She buried her face in his neck. He smelt of the sea and citrus fruits.

This silly little crush had no intentions of leaving did it? It was here to stay, stay and stay and stay until there was nothing left of her, until all her heart had been given to Dylan and even then it would grow into something too wild and foreign to be controlled or ignored.

Chapter 6

Monday, May 19th 2008

Fred Hollows High School, Brisbane

3:00 PM

Junie Bennett had a baby brother. Isaiah. It still felt odd to say it. Isaiah. She had a brother. Someone to split her lonely nights with, someone who could understand the hardship that came with being a Bennett.

Her mother had wanted to name him after her favourite celebrity or the latest baby name trends that listed all the fruits and colours. Junie had, of course, strongly opposed. She would not have her little brother named after a fruit or some sleazy celebrity. It was a week before the baby's birth that Dylan had suggested they name him after Audrey's eldest brother.

Junie's uncle -- Isaiah Bennett, along with Fiona Bennett -- was one of the two of Audrey's siblings that she actually liked. The other two, Johnny and Poppy, had been ghost figures she'd only heard about through snide comments from her mother. Uncle Zee lived just an hour outside Brisbane where he owned a small pub with his girlfriend of four years. He dropped by every now and then, took Junie to some fair or quirky restaurant in Greenslopes. Sometimes she could getaway with staying at his place for a couple of days (two weeks last summer) as Audrey pranced off with her own friends. He told the best stories, most of them wild tales about his youth and adventures he had on his holidays. Junie would listen with wide sparkling eyes and a wider smile.

Like every story, Uncle Zee's came to an end one night in a drunken brawl on cold, January night. Junie had cried for weeks, shut herself away and hid in the darkness to mourn his loss. Dylan - stupid, brilliant Dylan - had sought her out each time, followed her into the darkness and pulled her back before she fell into the abyss.

So, when he'd brought up the idea to name her new brother after her mad and magnificent uncle, Junie couldn't say no. Audrey had had a rather strained relationship with her brother but she, thankfully, had agreed with the name choice if only as a homage to him.

Of course life was difficult at the moment, Isaiah cried in the middle of the night, making it incredibly hard to gain even a minute of sleep. Audrey had managed to hold a job at the local shopping centre but the hours were long and the pay was low, and so Junie was often left with caring for Isaiah.During school, Audrey was able to drop Isaiah off at her Aunt Fiona's house for a while and pick him up at around five.

"Junie," Ms. Hammersmith said, wrenching her out of her contemplative thoughts.

She looked up, blinked, "Yeah?"

Ms. Hammersmith stared at her expectantly, "Well, answer the question."

Junie blinked again. She had zoned out again. Although, it wasn't her fault. Ms. Hammersmith had this unique ability to turn even the most exciting subjects into utter boring drivel. Which was ridiculous because to Junie, astronomy, was the most fascinating thing in existence yet Ms Hammersmith succeeded in painting it a thousand shades of grey.

She remembered the exact moment her fascination with the stars had first ignited in her. Junie had been in the back yard, stood in the shed searching for something to hold the hefty spider that inhabited her bedroom. Not to kill it. It had done no harm to her, so why kill it?

No, Junie wanted to examine it. Spiders were beautiful but deadly little things, she wanted a closer look. Five minutes into her search and she had been close to giving up when she came across a telescope.

It was quite large, coloured a dark gold and plastered in a layer of dust. Quickly forgetting the spider, Junie had grabbed the telescope and dragged it out of the shed and onto the grassy ground in the back yard.

Later that night when the sun had gone and the sky turned black, Junie had returned. She had looked through the telescope and saw an ocean of inky blackness had overtaken the once bright sky. It was that moment, that instant that Junie Bennett had fallen in love with the vast and endless blackness above. She had never seen anything so enchanting.

"Sorry, what was the question again?" Junie asked.

"At least ninety-five per cent of the celestial information we receive is in the form of light," Ms. Hammersmith said, "What information can scientist gain from the light?"

Junie pondered the question for a few moments before opening her mouth to speak.

"Well, the light information can be about the object's temperature, chemical surface gravity, shape, and structure," she began, "roughly eight-five per cent of the information in light is uncovered by using spectroscopy."

Ms. Hammersmith nodded and turning away from Junie she continued her long lecture on electromagnetic radiation. It was then that a piece of crumpled paper was flung onto her desk. Junie picked it up and evenly spread the paper out.

You're such a geek, Junebug, the note read.

Junie instantly recognised the messy handwriting and glanced back to look at the blue-eyed boy sat two rows behind her. Dylan grinned mischievously at her and he mouthed Dork, in return Junie mouthed Loser.

3:30 PM

"Are you coming to the skate park?" Dylan asked as the two friends headed out of the classroom. That lesson had dragged. It was as if time literally slowed down as soon you entered it.

Junie nodded, "definitely."

They turned a corner and entered a narrow corridor that was lined with orange lockers. It was filled with dozens of students, all milling about chatting and squawking away at whatever dilute matters that concerned their daily lives. Junie stopped before her locker and turning the dial, she yanked the door open.

She reached in and pulled out the skateboard Dylan had given her for her fourteenth birthday. It was much better than her last one; the old one had rickety wheels and chipped wood. This one was much lighter and easier to control and move when performing tricks.

A few lockers to her right, Dylan pulled out his skateboard. As they trudged out of the hallway, Junie dropped her skateboard onto the floor, and hopping on, she grinned and cried, "Race you! Last one to the skate park buys the milkshakes!"

Dylan immediately accepted her challenge and the two friends began their avid race. Teachers and students scolded them as they skated through the corridors and out of the school gates onto the hot afternoon streets of Brisbane. The cool wind whipped her flaming hair from eyes, the rush of the ride cooling and energising her.

She was grinning, pushing forward and jumping over obstacles, solely focused on winning. Dylan was laughing and it was such a lovely sound that she almost crashed into an elderly woman. At one point, it looked like Dylan was going to win but Junie managed regain her momentum and swerving a lamppost, she was able to pick up her speed and beat him.

"Another win for Bennett!" She announced, hands in the air as they rolled into the skate park.

"Whatever," he said rolling his eyes but he was grinning brightly.

Junie laughed. In the beginning, she had bought a skateboard because it was only five dollars at the local market, but then as the years went on, she found just how exhilarating skateboarding was and just how much she loved it. Every week, she and Dylan would travel down to the local skate park, where they would spend a few hours practising some tricks and joking around with the other skateboarders.

"Hey guys!" someone shouted.

Junie and Dylan glanced up. A tall and skinny blonde-haired boy was sat one of the elevated slopes.

"Hey Benja," Junie said with a smile.

Pushing himself up, he hopped onto his skateboard and slid down the slope to join the two friends on the ground. He fell into step with them as they made their way to the centre of the skate park. If you asked Junie, she really couldn't be sure of when or how she and Dylan had become friends with Benja Pasternak.

It may have been to do with the fact that Jake Ramsay had moved thousands of miles away to Perth almost a year ago today. In his absence Benja had changed. For better of course, he wasn't as vindictive and violent as he used to be. Without Jake around, Benja was quite an entertaining boy.

"So," Benja said, "are you guys going to the bonfire party tonight on Pandanus Beach?"

Junie glanced at her best friend, "are you going?"

Dylan lifted the cap from his head, and lazily raking a hand through his short dark locks, he placed cap back to front and shrugged. "I am, if you are."

As the familiar warmth swirled into her stomach, Junie found herself annoyed at how just simple words like that could cause just a reaction in her. Junie ignored the feelings of course, she had always been good at hiding how she truly felt. It was then that Sid Unwin decided to challenge Junie to some matches, she eagerly accepted and once again proved that even though she may have been one of the few girl skaters here but she was definitely not one to be messed with.

7:28 PM

The annual bonfire party on Pandanus Beach was in full swing.

A loud sigh escaped Junie Bennett's lips as she slumped down onto the soft bed of sand. Junie drew her knees in against her and wrapping her arms around them around them, she placed her chin between. Why had she even turned up? Not even five minutes after they had arrived and Dylan had rushed off to talk to Helen Torres and to think she had tried to look girly for this stupid thing. She had freed her hair from its ponytail; it framed her heart shaped face and flowed loosely down her back in fiery waves.

She wanted to make Dylan stop seeing her as just a friend; she needed Dylan to start noticing she was a bloody girl. That's why she was wearing this skirt. A skirt for God's sake and Dylan hadn't even blinked when he'd seen her.

Junie watched as Helen flirted with her best friend. She smiled up at him, batting her eyelashes and nodded at something he said. Junie wasn't sure whether she was going to threw up or scream. She wanted to take Dylan as far away from Helen as possible. That idiot. That stupid idiot. What did he see in her anyway?

God. It wasn't fair. It wasn't right. Things were changing too fast for to stop them. The popular kids like Helen Torres, Perry Han and CJ Leggero were circling around Dylan. They watched him, his fluid movements, the way his brought a room to life and his easy smiles. They watched Junie too and they didn't understand what he saw in her. He was stuck in the dirt when he could be running with the stars.

Junie tore her eyes away from the pair and looked over at the large bonfire circled by rings of stone and fed by broken branches. A dozen or more teenagers were crowded around the fire with drinks in their hands and laughter sparking between them. Maybe it would be better if she just went home. She wanted to see her little brother. She liked to watch him sleep, hear his soft breaths and that cute little face he made every now and then.

"Junie."

Junie looked up to find dressed in a plaid shirt, ripped jeans and converses.

"What? Did Helen get bored of you?" She asked, trying to keep her voice as steady as possible.

"No. She was just saying hi," he said, one corner of his mouth rose into one of his awkward but oddly endearing smiles.

He stepped closer and into the light of the fire. His blue eyes seemed to shine in the firelight and her heart skipped in response.

Dylan had sprung up last winter, now standing just an inch taller than Junie at five foot eight and probably still growing. Now that they were in high school, he had joined the school's swimming team and unsurprisingly become star member. Swimming had removed the softness from his body, it had grown hard and broad and she didn't know what to think of it. On top of that, after first term he came back with a deeper, huskier voice and she'd been so surprised to hear it she'd tripped over her own shoes. Dylan had laughed and his laugh hadn't changed per say it wasn't a little deeper but it still sounded like sunlight. Well, how she imagined sunlight to sound.

The evening breeze swam by, causing his black hair to flutter for a moment, before it fell in messy waves back over his forehead. As he stood there, gazing into her eyes and making her heart drum violently against her chest, she couldn't help thinking how he was gorgeous.

Junie looked away and cleared her throat and begged her heart to calm down. She looked up at the dimming purple sky. Dylan sighed softly and knelt down before her, closer than she expected but as not close as she wanted him to be.

"Here," he said.

When Junie looked over at him, he was holding a scarf in his hands. He chuckled at her confusion."It's your birthday present."

"Thank you," she said. Junie stared at Dylan, captured by his too-blue eyes as he leaned forward and slowly placed the scarf around her neck.

And then he did something to set her whole body alight.

Dylan pressed his lips onto her forehead and ripped her breath from her lungs. The army of frenzied butterflies was unleashed in her stomach as they travelled upward, coursing through her body and leaving lightheaded and jittery. His soft lips lingered for a few seconds before he pulled away.

"Happy birthday Junie," he smiled and it reminded her of a supernova.

For the longest moment all she could do was stare at him with a slack jaw and reddened cheeks.

"Dylan, I–I need to tell you s–something," she stammered.

"Yeah?"

She had to tell him. She had to tell him how crazy she was about him. She had to tell him that she didn't want to be just his friend anymore.

She had to tell him how badly she wanted to hold him and never let him go. She had to tell him how she would do anything just hold his hand.

She had to.

"Thanks for the scarf," she said, "I love it."

Chapter 7

Tuesday, May 19th 2009

Fortitude Valley, Brisbane

6:22 PM

"Zee," she let out an exasperated huff, "will you stop squirming?"

The little brown-eyed toddler was giggling and clapping his small chubby hands in glee. For the past thirty minutes Junie had been trying to feed her younger brother but every time the spoonful of porridge came his way he would wriggle and turn his head away.

Scooping up some porridge with the spoon, Junie hovered it in front of his mouth but as expected he refused. He was being difficult and she suspected he was enjoying this. This had not been Junie's plans for her Tuesday evening.

After school, she had planned to go to the skate park with Dylan but Audrey needed her to babysit Isaiah because she had dumped with a night shift at the store. She wouldn't be back home until eleven. She sighed and dropped the spoon back into the bowl of porridge. She stared at her little brother for a long moment.

"Fine, you don't want any? Then I'll have it," she said, scooping up some of the porridge and popping it into her mouth. A sharp and tangy flavour attacked her tongue and her face scrunched up at the disgusting taste.

Spluttering and coughing, Junie grabbed Isaiah's cup and guzzled down the milk. Her brother laughed, eyes alight with glee as he clapped his chubby hands erratically. Junie glanced at the bowl of porridge with a repulsed grimace, "God, that's disgusting. No wonder you don't like it."

This baby food, no matter how disgusting, was the cheapest they could afford

Times were hard, to be honest, times were always hard for the Bennetts. Audrey had been demoted from Assistant Manager to Store Clerk because the boss had caught Audrey giving sixty percent discounts to her friends. They were living off the small pool of money in both Junie's and Audrey's bank account and that wasn't going to last long.

Junie was already balancing schoolwork and a waitressing job at the cafe on Wickham Street. Taking care of Isaiah plus studying for school was beginning to take its toll. But, what else could she do? As her uncle had always told her, when life handed you lemons, you throw them right back. You kept moving and you didn't stop no matter how much weight you had to carry.

Junie was pulled out of her thoughts at the sound of the house phone ringing. She told Isaiah to at least try a bit of the porridge, before she left kitchen and came into the living room She went to the small table by the window and picked up the phone.

"Junebug!" Dylan greeted on the other line.

Junie smiled in spite of herself. It was stupid and probably unhealthy, but even though she had seen him only three hours ago, she missed the idiot. "What is it?"

"Come to my place," he said.

"Why?"

"Today's your sixteenth! It's your birthday and we are going to celebrate!"

"New Zealand," Junie sighed, "I can't. My mum's not here, I have to take care of Zee."

"Bring him with you then," he said matter-of-factly.

She paused, humming in thought as she contemplated his offer.

"Junie, c'mon, I have a little surprise for you," Dylan coaxed, "It's your sweet sixteen, I can't let you spend your sweet sixteenth by yourself. So, I'll see you in an hour?"

She sighed once more, like she could ever deny Dylan Mercer of anything. She nodded, "Oh, Okay then, see ya."

She ended the call and rushed back into the kitchen, not too surprised to find Isaiah had the porridge splattered all over him, the little minx had threw the bowl onto the floor. Shaking her head, she removed his bib. She bopped his nose, a habit she had picked up from Dylan, and he giggled.

"Come on Zee," she said, "We're going out!"

From the unpleasant smell, Junie guessed he needed his diaper changed. She sung and made comical faces to distract him as she cleaned his bottom and took him to the bathroom to bathe him. He kept splashing water at her face, laughing at her annoyance when he did so.

Once she dressed him, she set him down on the floor, facing him away from her and gave him some toys to play with. Junie quickly tore off her shirt and skinny jeans and zoomed into the bathroom, where she had a speedy shower. She came back, stumbling to her wardrobe and desperately began searching for something to wear.

Her clothes either needed washing or they weren't nice enough. If she had the money, she would have brought new ones. Junie soon spotted a black dress peeking out from a pile of suitcases. She trudged towards them and forcibly yanked it out. Junie stumbled back and fell to the floor.

She groaned, pushing herself back up, she observed the piece of clothing at arm's length. Hm, pretty. It was a knee-length yellow dress that actually looked like it had already been washed.

The last time she had worn it was three years ago at her grandfather's funeral. She frowned, wondering if the dress would still fit her but when she did slip into it, it fit perfectly. Junie wondered whether she should be dressing in the clothes she had worn to a funeral.

"Doesn't matter," she muttered.

It wasn't as if she had any other washed clothes to wear. Junie opened the drawers of her dresser and threw on several bracelets. She quickly slipped into some white converses and as she quickly tied her shoelaces, she glanced at the clock. It was already twenty to seven.

She looked at her reflection in the long mirror and carefully styled her hair up into a neat bun. Three years ago, Junie would have scoffed at the idea of wearing make-up but that was three years ago and this was now and her views of a lot things had changed since then.

She didn't know why but she had started wearing make-up, she just knew she wanted to look pretty for a change. Not a lot, just some mascara and eyeliner. Junie loved liquid eyeliner, one of the best things invented. She sat on the edge of the bed and applied the mascara and liquid eyeliner. There was no point in denying it, Junie wanted to look pretty for Dylan, she needed that idiot to start seeing her as a girl.

Once she was ready, she picked up Isaiah and placing him in his pram, they left the house.

7:18 PM

"You took your sweet arse time didn't you?" Dylan said as Junie walked into the back garden.

She didn't respond, she just stared in wonder at the sight before her. Dylan was sat on a picnic bench that was adorned with all flowers and ribbons and it was set with all sorts of sweets, sandwiches, and a great big white cake that was situated in the middle of the table. There were candles situated all around them, lighting up the dark garden and giving everything a magical glow.

"Dylan," she breathed, "Did you do this?"

He grinned, "Yeah, do you like it?"

All she could do was nod because she couldn't even begin to find the words to express just how much she liked it. Like, wasn't the correct word to use.

"How did you do all this?"

"My sisters helped," he replied.

"This, this...is amazing, Dyl."

"Well, no use standing around," he laughed, "Come on."

Junie held her brother against her hip as she walked over to the picnic bench and sitting down next to Dylan, she placed Isaiah on her lap.

"Good evening, Zee," Dylan said, bopping the little boy's nose and causing him to giggle. "Let's eat!"

Junie did not hesitate. The two friends laughed and joked as they ate the food that had been prepared. Dylan even managed to coax little Isaiah into eating too. Her brother was devouring the plate of spring rolls, he wasn't spitting or throwing any of his food.

This. Junie thought, this right here, was perfect. She was with two most important people in her life on her birthday.

Dylan finished his bottle of coke and placing it on the table, he stood up. He walked to the other side and picking up his acoustic guitar from underneath, he walked back round to stand before her, "Here's a little something I wrote."

"Hey you, I heard it's your birthday, and I just wanted to say, I'm so glad it's your birthday," he smiled at her then, "and I just wanted to say. I'm so glad it's your birthday."

The guitar strings danced along with his voice, crisp and syrupy. Her heart drummed to the beat.

"I'll make your loneliness fade away. Just hold my hand, and everything will be okay. As long as you have me, I swear you will never feel like yesterday".

Each time his eyes – blue, blue, blue, always too blue – landed on her and it felt like the whole world was collapsing around her and it was just the two of them, floating in the blue darkness.

"Hey you, I heard it's your birthday, and I just wanted to say, I'm so glad it's your birthday, and I just wanted to say. I'm so glad it's your birthday."

He was grinning at her now and butterflies swarmed her stomach and erupted into every crevice of her body. His voice, so sweet, sweet like honey and all the ice cream they used to eat until their brains froze.

"And I am here to say, to scream at the top of my lungs, so the whole world can hear me now. Happy birthday to you."

The air in her lungs had frozen at the last note of the song and crickets rode on the silence that followed. It was only broken by the sound of Isaiah clapping and giggling.

"Dylan," she gasped, "I...I...that was amazing."

Red bloomed over his cheeks and Junie held Isaiah closer to stop herself from jumping up to kiss him. He shuffled on his feet, fingers drumming on the wooden body of the guitar as he gave her that lopsided grin she liked too much.

"Th-thanks, Junebug," he said.

She couldn't look away, too hypnotised to anything else. He looked gorgeous like that, dark hair fell across his forehead in tousled waves, cheeks red and mouth parted in a bright smile.

Dylan stared at her, his gaze boring into hers. He cocked his head and she was reminded of a puppy, "Junie, are you okay?."

She couldn't stop the words that came out next, they were rising and ascending inside of her, bubbling until they finally slipped out, "I like you."

"Aw," Dylan rubbed the back of his neck, "I like you too."

"N-no...No...I mean...I like you," she said, "like, I don't want to be your friend Dylan. I-I want..."

She wanted everything and nothing less. Junie knew her face was now a beetroot red and she felt so light-headed, her heart drumming hard in her chest. Dylan blinked. His eyes slowly narrowing and she could see it. She could see the cogs turning, the wires connecting as the realisation dawned on him.

"You like me," he said in a strangely flat tone.

She should take it back. She should just laugh and say it was a joke but she didn't do that. Junie just looked him straight in the eyes, determined to get this over and done with, "Yes."

She really didn't know or understand where this new-found courage had come from but she was not about to question it either. He stared at her, his eyes wide and mouth slightly agape, a red blush painting his cheeks and he hadn't said anything in so long.

Junie pulled Isaiah against her chest. "Well, say something."

Dylan's grip on the guitar tightened. "Junie," he swallowed. "You know you're my best friend, the best I've ever had and I-I love you, I do but...but..."

When he looked back up at her, she knew he didn't have to say anything because the sad slant of his mouth told her a hundred stories. It sent a knife sinking slowly into her heart.

"But not in that way," she whispered.

Even Isaiah sensed the tensed atmosphere; he sat in silence with his thumb in mouth looking back and forth between the two.

"Junie–"

A laugh tore its way out of her mouth. It sounded fake and tinny to her ears. "Dylan, calm down...I'm fine, you're acting like I was stabbed."

"Junie–"

"Dylan, I'm fine," She said forcing a smile, "Now, could we please just cut the cake? I'm starving."

He looked at her for the longest moment, his face unreadable before he nodded. "Okay, I'll go get the knife then."

He pulled the guitar strap up and over his head and placed the guitar on the floor. He cast her one last look and walked back into the house.

Junie swallowed a lump in her throat she was sure was her heart. She tipped her head back and closed her eyes to stop the tears from spilling.

"I'm fine, I'm fine, I'm fine."

She was fine. She was good. She was brilliant. Better than ever.

"I'm fine, I'm fine, I'm - God," she bit her lip. Junie stood up, dropped Isaiah back into his pram, grabbed her things and escaped before she could mess anything else up.

Chapter 8

W ednesday, May 19th 2010

Kangaroo Point, Brisbane

5:56 PM

As she slipped out of the kitchen and onto the patio in the back garden, Junie Bennett noted the chill in the afternoon. The sky had been coated with thick clouds that refused to let the sun through and cast a shade of dull grey on the city.

A gust of air rushed past her, causing her fiery hair to lift and dance in the frosty wind. She placed a cigarette between her rosy lips and digging a hand into in her inner jacket pocket, she pulled out the small lighter. She pursed her lips as she rolled the wheel of the lighter down with her thumb, a click sounded and an orange flame came to life. Covering her hand over the flame and protecting it from the blowing wind, Junie placed the tip of the cigarette into the fire and watched as it burnt.

After a few seconds, she let the flame die and stuffed the lighter back in her pocket. She held onto the cigarette with two fingers and sucked in the smoke, drawing it into her lungs and the intoxicating warmth coursed through her. She could feel the nervousness and stress that had plagued her all day, melt and dissipate as the smoke swirled in her lungs.

She pulled the cigarette from her mouth and slowly blew, watching as a cloud of smoke escaped from her lips. There was nothing like a cigarette to calm her after a stressful day. Junie sighed in relief. She brought the cigarette back to her lips and sucked in the smoke, she leaned back against the wall. She lazily took drags of her cigarette as she looked up at the sky, thoughts and concerns drifting through her mind.

At sixteen – well, seventeen today – Junie knew she should not be smoking. She knew all the hazards, she had seen all the posters and understood the consequences but she didn't care. Lately, Junie had been finding it hard to care about anything.

She had only been smoking for a little over six months now. Junie Bennett would say she had all the reasons in the world to smoke.

What, with her best and only friend – who she may or may not have been in love with – dating the school's It Girl. With her mother rarely home and always out to God knows where. With her little brother making a full recovery from a case of meningitis that had scared her to death. And with two jobs and having to balance schoolwork she was already behind on, Junie Bennett would say she had every damn right under the sun to smoke as much as she pleased.

Behind her she heard the door open and footsteps approaching before she saw her aunt come to stand beside her.

Fiona Bennett shook her head, frowning in disapproval at the sight of her niece smoking. "That's really bad for you."

Junie sucked in the smoke, inhaling deeply and exhaled, "I know."

"Zee looks better," she said, "Thank God the meningitis has finally cleared up."

Junie simply nodded, choosing not to think about how ill her little brother had been in the past few weeks. As always, Dylan been there to support her, hold her and keep her from crumbling down. Dylan. She sucked on the cigarette.

She didn't how she would have coped or what would have happened if he hadn't been there. After Isaiah had been discharged from the hospital Junie had decided the best place for him to be for a while would be at their aunts. Fiona would take care of him when she was at school or work.

"Your friend called," Fiona told her, "Dylan, he wants to see you."

"Thanks."

Later, after she had finished her cigarette and ate the lemon meringue her aunt had made, Junie rushed up to the bathroom. Dylan thought she had quit smoking a month ago and not wanting him to think otherwise, she brushed her teeth and sprayed away the smell of smoke with some of Fiona's flowery scented fragrances. Before she left, Junie crept into her aunt's bedroom where Isaiah slept soundly in his cot. She ran a hand through his tousled blonde hair and leaning down, she placed a soft kiss onto his forehead.

5:50 PM

"So how's school, darling?" Georgia Mercer, Dylan's mother, asked as Junie entered the house.

Ever since Lena and Bethany had left for university last year the house had become quieter, less hectic. She kind of missed the sound of Bethany's gleeful laugh and Lena's quick, witty replies.

Junie dropped her skateboard next to the coat hunger and shrugged, "Same as always...terrible."

"Aw it'll get better, you're graduating next year, " Georgia gave her a warm smile, "Dyl's in his room."

Junie nodded and starting up the stairs.

"Oh Junie," Georgia said.

Junie paused and glanced back, "Yeah?"

"Happy birthday, love," she said with the softest smile that was so much like Dylan's.

Junie smiled back, "Oh...thank you."

She turned and ran up the last of the steps. Dylan's room was the second door to the right. Like always, she never bothered to knock, only barged in with an easy smile and a quip ready on her lips. It felt different this time. It was the first time she'd been to his house in two months and for the first time in years, Junie felt out of place. They didn't see much of each other lately. Dylan had the swim team and soccer practice, when he wasn't doing that Helen would whisk him away. Junie had to work at the cafe, take care Dylan and study for all the extra classes she'd signed up for.

Her heart beat too fast as her eyes landed on him fast asleep on his bed. Funnily enough it was the sight of the mess, the clothes everywhere and the sound of Beatles playing quietly in the background that calmed her down.

Junie walked over to his bed, her hand came to rest on the head board as she gazed down at him. She bit her lip. His black hair stuck up from all angles, his parted slightly as he snored.

It had been a hard year. Ever since she'd confessed that night in his garden, things had been - strained to say the least. In the following months it had been so hard to be around him without her heart breaking. She'd avoided him, spent her days in the lost in physics work, charting galaxies and the death of stars with the tip of her finger. Just as she'd feared Dylan began dating Helen Torres at Christmas, apparently they'd kissed at Perry Han's house party and had been the golden couple ever since.

Dylan's eyebrows knitted together. He scowled and muttered something she couldn't catch. Junie rubbed his cheek with her thumb and the scowl melted away. Her breath hitched as she wondered if she had done that.

She'd been so desperate for him to forget her confession, she faced him with a bright grin and told him she was happy he'd found someone. She was either a good actress or Dylan didn't want to push the subject. On the bright side, their relationship - whatever it was or whatever was left of it - had started to click back together, piece by piece.

Dylan's eyes fluttered open, it took a few seconds before they focused on her. Junie quickly pulled her hand from his cheek.

"Junie...?" He grumbled.

"Hey," she said softly, "Are you alright?"

Dylan rose up onto his elbows and let out a wince.

"My head's killing me," he said, his voice deep and raspy.

Junie slid onto the space next to him on the bed, pulling up her legs so she sat crossed legged. She frowned. "Why haven't you been to school in like two days, New Zealand? Are you moping about because of your break-up with Helen?"

He pushed himself up to sit and leaned back against the headboard. He sniffed, "I think I'm getting a cold and I, sort of, sprained my ankle."

Junie cocked an eyebrow. "What? How?"

Dylan pulled the duvet covers aside, revealing his left leg that was dressed in a white cast. "Y'know how Sid Unwin is an arsehole?"

Junie nodded. Everybody knew that.

"Well, I was at the skate park and he bet that I couldn't do a rail side," he said and he looked so adorably sheepish about it all, "And, well....obviously I lost the bet."

She laughed. "You're an idiot."

His mouth stretched into a grin, wide and cheeky, his blue eyes finding hers as he said, "That's why you love me."

She looked at him with obvious want, "I do."

The words floated in the space between them, taunting her. Dylan's eyes widened and Junie wanted nothing more than to jump out of the window.

"Um."

"Junie."

"I'm sorry. I just meant that...you're an idiot...and you ...you..."

"Junie."

"You're just so - so you, how could I not? And I-"

"Juniper!" He snapped and she jumped. He sighed, his shoulders sagging. When he said her name again, it was too soft for her to bear. "Juniper."

On him, her name sounded like a melody, like a treasure he couldn't afford to lose. She bit her lip and braced herself for the inevitable rejection. The first time had broken her heart and she was still recovering. The second time would not shatter it, it would cause it to vanish, leaving nothing but an empty space where her heart used to be. She squared her shoulders and braced herself. She would bear the empty space because she had to. Perhaps life would be easier without it.

Instead, he said, "I've missed you."

She blinked. "What?"

"I miss you," he said, this time his eyes met hers. "We haven't been hanging out or even talking in the last year and I miss you, Junie, I miss you and I..."

Junie waited with her heart, her lungs, her stomach sat in her throat.

"You what?" she choked out.

"I miss you," he said again, his eyes flitted to the ceiling, to the window and then finally back to her. "I miss you and I love you, Junie."

The words shot out like arrows and pierced Junie's chest. He continued to speak and more arrows came, each one lodged into her heart with sparks.

"I want to be your friend, I do, but I also I want more, I want...I want you," he said, "I love you like I hope you love me."

"Dylan," she whispered.

"If you'll have me," he said, looking at her with those big blue eyes. He leaned into her, "If you'll have me, Junie. I'll be yours."

Her breathing had become ragged, her heart was a beating wild thing punctured by forty buzzing arrows.

"And - and if you we don't work out?" she asked, her gaze dropped to his mouth and he drew in the sharpest breath.

Junie watched his mouth form the words. "We will," he said.

"But how do you know?"

He leaned closer and closer and pressed a soft, silky kiss to her cheek. Sparks popped where his lips met her reddened skin. "I don't," he whispered as he dragged his mouth up her cheek and onto her forehead where he pressed another kiss, "and you don't either, Junebug."

Her body vibrated and sang at each kiss he placed to her other cheek, her nose, her eyebrow.

"And Helen?" she asked, forcing herself - despite everything she wanted - to pull back and look at him, "What...what about Helen?"

They'd broke up a few weeks ago. It wasn't much of a surprise, for the past year Dylan and Helen had a confusing on-off relationship nobody could work out. One week, all they would be doing was arguing and rumours fly around that Fred Hollows High's golden couple had split, but the next week they were together again, kissing by the lockers, holding hands to class.

"Junie. Junie. She's not you," his slid hand to grasp the back of her neck, "Last year, I know I hurt you when I said I didn't the feel same but it's only because I didn't understand, Junie. I didn't get it. I do now. I thought it was normal for your heart to beat for someone and only them. I didn't wake up and realise I love you. Junie, I've always loved you and that's why I never realised it because I've never known anything other than - than... this."

Her eyes were wide and she had grabbed his shirt at some point. "Dylan."

"So," he said, resting his forehead against hers. "What do you say?"

"To what?" her voice barely more than a squeak.

"To us," he whispered. "You and me."

She nodded, too stunned to say anything else and there it was. That all-consuming smile, the birth of a universe, shooting light into every cell of her body and leaving her aglow.

"I would kiss you," he laughed and the sound rang through her, "but I think I have a cold."

Her gaze dropped down to his mouth again. She had never allowed herself the luxury before. It was always short, fleeting glances before Dylan or anyone could notice. She had waited almost five years for this moment and there was not a single chance in heaven or hell that she would wait a moment longer.

"I don't care," she breathed before she clenched both of her hands into his shirt and kissed him.

And it felt as if the scattered stars had finally aligned.

Chapter 9

Thursday, May 19th 2011

Wooloongabba, Brisbane

8:04 PM

When her shift ended, Junie pulled on her coat and said goodbye to Tulip and Cara. They gave her a small smile and waved back with a touch of exhaustion. She would see them again tomorrow afternoon at the same time.

Junie had managed to strike up a schedule with the boss about her hours at the cafe, it fit around her other job and her school . She quite liked waitressing at Lolita's, the hours were good, the pay was much better than her last job and she was friends with all the employees.

Junie sighed and stepped out into the breeze of the crispy night.She walked out of the back yard of the cafe and came to the main road, where she stood underneath a street lamp and waited for the rush of cars to stop so she could cross.

"Junebug!"

She spun around and when she found Dylan, leaning against the hood of his car she grinned. Junie started walking towards him but soon broke into a run. She wrapped her arms around his neck and pulled him into a tight hug. Dylan let out a surprised yelp and laughed, the sound warming her chest.

"Hey babe," He rested his hands on her hips and burying his face in her neck, he said, "How was work?"

Her body hummed at the feel of him pressed against her. A whole week. She had not seen Dylan for a whole week. Although that may not have seemed long but for Junie it felt like years. They had both been busy with the upcoming exams, college applications, school and just life in general.

Dylan pulled back to look at her, still grinning like a boy on Christmas morning before he leaned forward and kissed her. It was warm and sweet and sent electricity buzzing throughout her. She felt alive, her heart jumping in her chest as his mouth parted for her and he deepened the kiss. When she pulled away, Junie felt dizzy, lightheaded like she buzzed on alcohol. It was always felt good to see her boyfriend.

That still felt surreal to admit. She didn't think she was ever going to get used to that. She had wanted and wished for this —them —so long, that she hadn't thought it would ever come true. But it had, and it felt like a dream.

"So," Dylan said as they turned and hopped into his car. "It's your birthday today, there's a cute little restaurant not far from here and I thought it would be cool if we—"

"No."

Dylan glanced at her, "What?"

It had been a long day and to be truthful, Junie was absolutely exhausted. For the past two weeks Junie had, what felt like, an endless series of exams. Everything had been so stressful. It was hard trying to balance, exam revision, work and looking after her little brother. She was thankful that her aunt was always on hand to help.

Fiona babysat Isaiah most of the time. So, it gave Junie the time and space she needed to properly concentrate and study meticulously for the infinite list of exams she had. Next Thursday Junie had her most imperative exam of all. Advanced Astronomy and out of all her subjects, that was the one she had studied the hardest and most thoroughly for. She needed to get the top grade if she wanted to pursue a career in Astronomy.

"Sorry, I'm just so tired, I've literally only had, like, four hours sleep these past few weeks," she said, "These exams have just been stressing me out so much, I just.. .wanna go home and sleep."

"I understand," he said but she could hear the touch of disappointment in his voice, "But I am definitely taking you out tomorrow."

She gave him a wearily smile, "Okay."

Junie would have loved to go to one of those night clubs and just drink and dance her worries away. Why not? It was her birthday today. Her eighteenth to be exact. She had been looking forward to this day for a long time and the fact that she was too tired to celebrate was rather disheartening. As he started the car, Dylan leant forward and dropped a soft kiss on her forehead. She grinned widely at the warm touch of his lips.

9:15 PM

Crying.

A whole lot of crying and a whole lot of shouting.

That was the first thing Junie and Dylan heard upon entering her house. Junie frowned as she followed the noise that led her into kitchen. She found Isaiah stood by the stove with his tears streaming down his face and mouth wide open as he wept. Audrey was glaring down at him, shouting and telling him to stop being so ridiculous. And then there was the sound smack of Audrey's hand hitting the little boy's cheek and there was the stunned silence that followed.

Audrey glared down at her son, "Zee, you need to learn to behave! When I say no, I mean no. You need to stop acting like spoilt brat and learn some manners. Now go to your room!"

Isaiah's hand went up to his cheek that was quickly turning red, he sniffled as he nodded numbly. Junie and Dylan stared, eyes wide as they gaped at the scene before them. Junie was shocked, frozen for a split second and she felt something inside her snap. Snap and ignite and release a wave of boiling wrath. Her eyes were like laser beams as she glared hotly at her mother.

"Dyl," she said through gritted teeth, "Take Zee outside."

Dylan didn't need to be told twice. He threw a worried glance at his girlfriend, before he nodded and walked over to Isaiah. The little blonde-haired boy was snivelling. Dylan picked him up, holding him close as he hurried out of the kitchen

Silence reined for the longest moment, Junie took a deep breath. She stepped forward, anger bubbling inside her.

"You hit him," she said. It wasn't a question, it was a simple and icy cold fact. "You actually hit Isaiah. What the hell is wrong with you?"

Audrey grimaced, "Calm down."

This, of course, did the exact opposite. In fact, it only made Junie angrier. Angrier than she had ever been in her entire life. This was almost fourteen years of pent-up frustration, disappointment and anger releasing itself all at once.

"Calm down?" She repeated, utterly aghast, "Calm down?"

"Yes, calm down."Audrey grabbed a bottle of whiskey from cupboard and removing the lid, she took a swig of it. "Look, he wanted some candy and you know how candy gets him hyper and I told him no but he kept demanding and crying and screaming and I was just so tired, I lost control alright?"

Junie's hands clenched into tights fists and she had to take several steps back to stop herself from hitting something or rather someone.

"No," she breathed, the wrath she felt seeping into of her tone, "It's not alright. It's never alright. You don't hit him. He's three years old, you do no hit a child! You do not hit your son!"

"Look!" Audrey snapped, mirroring Junie's intense glare. "You don't know how hard it's been for me. OK? I work for long hours and when I get home all I'm met with is bills, bills, some more bills!"

"Are you kidding me?!" Junie bellowed. "Audrey, you quit every job you get after two weeks! You're never home, you're always out with one of your new boyfriends, partying and drunk out of your mind! And the rare times that you are home, you're drunk! Drunk or asleep! Do you know how many times social services has been here? Thirteen! Thirteen bloody times and each time I've lied for you."

"I—"

"No," she snapped, she couldn't stop the words that spilled out, "You claim that you work hard? You claim that you're a mother? That's the biggest load of bullshit I have ever heard! You have and will never have any right to be called a mother! You lost that right a long time ago. Even before Isaiah was born, you were never there for me! I had to look after myself! For God's sake I had to look after you!"

Audrey took another swig from the whiskey bottle. "Did you know I was model when I was younger? I worked for the best designer labels, I was on my way to being the top model in Australia but then I had this stupid one night stand and I found out pregnant with you. I could have earned millions, seen so many places but no, I ended up being stuck in this squalor little house with no job and barely any money."

"Are...Are you blaming me for how your life turned out?" Junie's gasped, "That's it, I can't do this anymore. I'm done!"

"Done?"

"Yes, done!" She shouted, "I've had enough of you! All these years I've praying and hoping you would change,

that you would stop drowning your sorrows and problems in smoking, partying and alcohol. But I'm done! I'm
done with you! I'm leaving!"

"What?" Audrey spat.

"You heard me!" She snapped, "I'm eighteen years of
age now and I don't have to stay here any longer, I'm
leaving and I'm taking Isaiah with me!"

"And where are you gonna go?" Audrey sneered, her
tone so infuriatingly mocking, "Who do you have Junie?"

10:48 PM

"Here," Dylan said as he passed the glass of orange
juice and sat down beside her.

"Thanks," she murmured. It was times like this that
orange juice, no matter how nice, would not suffice. It
was times like this that Junie felt the urge to smoke. She
hadn't had a single cigarette in almost three months and
she was planning to keep it that way, no matter how
much the situation or her mood demanded it.

Junie remembered how Audrey had simply stared
blankly, doing nothing as she grabbed Isaiah and
stormed out of the house. She didn't even care. She
could not go back there. She just couldn't. Junie took a
deep breath and bringing the glass cup to her lips, she
gulped down the juice.

She felt tears sting her eyes and she blinked, willing
them away.

"Junie, I..." Dylan began, the pain evident in his tone, "I'm sorry."

She glanced at him and shook her head, "No, I'm sorry, I can't believe I put up with her for so long, I...I just...I thought she would change. I don't know what to do anymore. I'm done."

He slung his arm around her shoulders and pulling her against him, he kissed her forehead, "Everything's going to be fine."

She shuffled closer to him and rested her head on his shoulder. Dylan and Junie were sat in the living room of his house. As Junie had tried to regain her composure, Dylan had fed Isaiah and cheered him up. It wasn't long before the three-year-old became tired and Dylan had carried him up to Lena's old room where he was now soundly sleeping.

"Where are you gonna go?" Dylan asked after a beat of silence.

"My aunt's," she replied, "Fiona will take us in."

He gently squeezed her shoulder, "Junie."

"Yes?"

"She was wrong," he said softly, tucking a loose strand of her hair behind her ear, "When she said, you had no one, she was wrong. You have me, you'll always have me, Junebug."

"I know," Junie felt a smile tug at her lips as her eyes fell shut. She dropped her head onto his shoulder, "Thanks, New Zealand."

Chapter 10

S aturday, May 19th 2012

Ascot, Brisbane

8:13 AM

Junie sighed and lifting the duvet cover over her head, she tried to go back to sleep. However that attempt was disrupted at the sound of the door creaking open and her boyfriend trudging into the room. He shouted at the top of his lungs, his deep voice bellowing and shooting right through her as he told her to wake. She heard his footsteps storming over to the bed and he abruptly tore the covers off of her.

"Junebug," he said, "Rise and shine, it's time to get up."

She rolled onto her back and groaned, "Do I have to?"

He nodded, "Yep, you can't spend the rest of your life in bed."

"I can try," she grumbled. She blinked, her eyes fluttering open and meeting her boyfriend's expectant gaze. His eyes were bright and blue and there was a grin just as bright plastered on his face. She had always loved his eyes, so trusting and cheerful and bluer and deeper than any oceans. His dark hair was a coiled mess, sticking up in the most ridiculous way.

Junie's eyes slowly wandered down his bare torso to the grey sweatpants that slung dangerously low around his hips and she swallowed.

"When you've finished checking me out," he said, that grin morphing into an arrogant smirk, "you can get up."

Junie blushed. She lifted the pillow from underneath her and placed it over her face.

"Shut up," she mumbled and she heard him laugh, soft and melodious. The mattress creaked and lowered as she felt Dylan slide in beside her. He pulled the pillow away and shuffling closer, he pressed a soft kiss to her cheek.

"You're too cute, Juniper," he grinned.

"Dylan, you idiot," she chuckled as she kissed his cheek too.

"That's why you love me."

She grinned at him, "Yeah, it is."

He rolled on top of her, sinking them lower into the bed and grinned widely, "Happy birthday, Junie."

And with that he kissed her. It was light and tasted of all things sweet. She wrapped her arms around his neck and pulled him closer, she heard him let out a soft moan. Sugary warm currents of sunshine filled her mouth. The sweetness soon melted into a spreading warmth. And soon into a heart quickening heat as the kiss deepened and she buried her fingers in his messy dark hair. Their breathing was hard and shallow when they finally pulled apart.

"You should sleep here more often," he said.

She nodded in agreement, "Planning on it."

Dylan's parents had gone to some remote village in Ireland for two weeks. He had made the most of their absence by inviting Junie to spend the nights at his house. The sleepovers were just like the ones they had when they were kids with popcorn, sweets and action films except with some added flirting and kissing.

Sometimes, she wondered if he had done with this Helen when they had dated. She tried to push those thoughts away because they were stupid and irrational. She knew he wouldn't have. She could see it in the way he could barely contain his excitement when they were together. It was different. They were different.

"Well," he said licking his lips, "Can you sleep here tonight?"

She had a few essays to do but they were not due until next month. She ran her fingers through his hair, loving its silkiness. "I will, if you can tell me what day it is next Friday."

"Don't you mean today?" He said, "Today's your birth-day."

She shook her head, "No, I mean what day is it next Friday?"

Dylan did that impossibly cute thing where he furrowed his eyebrows and nibbled on his lower lip. "Oh," he chuckled, "It's our two year anniversary."

She smiled. Friday, May 25th would be the day that Dylan, during a date to the cinemas, had asked her to be his girlfriend. Along with Isaiah's first words and being accepted into Queensland University of Technology that had been one of the best moments of her life.

"Bingo!" She laughed, leaning up giving him a quick kiss.

"Guess what?" He said.

"What?"

It was such a shame Dylan had decided not to go to university. He'd wanted to pursue a career in music and university would not allow him to do so. At the moment, he had a job as a part time DJ for Nova 106. 9, it was one of Brisbane's top radio stations. He loved it, he was great friends with all his work colleagues, the hours were not long and the pay was good.

She remembered how ecstatic he had been when he had first received the job three months ago. For while he'd been worried that he would have to work at the call-centre for the rest of his life. He had saved up enough up money and was now planning to move out of his parent's house to his own apartment.

After weeks of searching he had finally found an affordable place to live. It was a rather small but lovely apartment in Auchenflower that he was more than ecstatic to move into.

"The radio station is letting me play a few of my songs," he said.

She gasped, "Really?"

"Yeah," he nodded eagerly.

She laughed and cupping his face, she pulled him into a kiss. A slow and lingering one that made her heart jump at the brilliant sensation of his mouth.

"That's amazing! I'm telling they are going to love your songs, New Zealand!" She said pulling away and grinning up at him, "Watch, this time next year, you'll be a singing sensation."

He blushed, "I wish."

He was so cute. She smiled, "New Zealand, I have to go to my lecture."

Junie Bennett loved life as a university student. It was a thousand times better than the torturous times of high school. There was a lot more freedom, it was not infested with as many idiots and although the lectures did last quite a few hours, Junie still loved it. Studying physics was both challenging and fascinating. Just how she liked it.

"When is it?"

"In about an hour," she answered.

"Well, let's think..." he said, pausing for a few seconds, "It'll take about ten minutes to have a shower, five minutes to get dressed and ten minutes to get to QUT."

She quirked an eyebrow, "So?"

"So, that leaves us with twenty-five minutes to spare," he said, a mischievous grin slowly creeping back onto his face. "What can we do in twenty-five minutes...twice?"

Junie spluttered, "Dylan!"

He laughed, "Don't pretend you don't want to."

"Shut up," she said with a roll of her eyes and patted his arm, "Right, get off me, I have to go."

Dylan rolled off of her and unceremoniously slumped down beside her. Junie hopped off the bed and checked the time on the clock nailed to the poster of the Beatles. Her chocolate brown eyes widened when she realised she didn't even have an hour, only thirty minutes.

"Crap," she hissed, "I'm going to be late!"

She rushed over to her duffel bag and immediately started yanking out some clothes. She threw them over head and landed on the bed where Dylan sat, watching his panicked girlfriend in amusement.

"It's not funny, Dyl!" She cried as she sped off into the bathroom. He only laughed.

She quickly tore off her pyjamas and hopped into the shower. Since she was running late, Junie decided to kill two birds with one stone by having a shower and brushing her teeth at the time.

It was not a bright idea but it was well known that Junie's brain never functioned well in the morning. It was soon proven why it was not a good idea when the shampoo foam slipped into her mouth and mixed with the toothpaste. It took Junie a good five minutes to remove the horrid taste from her mouth.

Fifteen minutes later, she found Dylan in the kitchen. She dropped a quick kiss on his forehead before she grabbed her bag and headed to the university.

7:25 PM

"Do you like it Junebug?" Isaiah asked.

Thanks to Dylan, that was all the four-year-old called her these days. Junie smiled down at the piece of paper her little brother had handed her.

"Is that me?" She asked, pointing to the stick figure in the middle.

Isaiah nodded, "Yeah and the other two are Auntie Fiona and Dylan."

Junie's smiled broadened.

"I didn't draw Mummy because she's never here," he said with a slight furrow of his eyebrows.

Fiona threw a concerned glance at Junie. She placed a hand on the little boy's shoulder and tentatively asked, "Are you bothered that she's never here, sweetie?"

Isaiah took a bite of the pepperoni pizza and shrugged, "Should I be?"

"Thanks for the picture, love," Junie said eager to change the subject, "It's brilliant, I think I might frame it."

Junie tried not to think about how she had not seen her mother for almost five months now. Fiona had informed Junie that Audrey had left. Where? She didn't know. Nobody knew. All the concise email that Junie received said was that Audrey was leaving with her friends.

To go where or do what was unclear. It was her nineteenth birthday, she was at her favourite restaurant, having a delicious dinner with four of the most important people in her life and she was going to enjoy it. She was not going to let Audrey ruin it for her. For the past year Junie and Isaiah had been living with their aunt in Kangaroo Point and rather happily she may add. She should have moved out earlier.

"You looking forward to tomorrow, Junie?" Farah beamed.

Tomorrow night, Junie was going clubbing to celebrate her nineteenth. It was going to be a night of drinking, dancing and debauchery with a group of her university friends. Junie was at first doubtful that she would make any friends at the university but she was wrong. She had made plenty including the ever wonderful Farah Finley.

The dark-haired and green-eyed girl came from Manchester in England and was in her second year, studying Psychology. She had a creative mind and impeccable fashion sense. She planned to start her own designer label, which Junie knew would be an instant success. Farah had become her closest friend. She was funny and loud and always managed to make Junie smile.

Junie nodded, "Definitely."

"Good, because there's this fantastic club in New Farm that you need to check out," Farah said in that strong English accent Junie adored so much.

She glanced at her boyfriend. Dylan's hand slid onto her thigh and as he squeezed it, he leaned forward and kissed her softly.

"Happy birthday Junie," he smiled.

She could feel her cheeks burning, "Thanks New Zealand."

Chapter 11

S unday, May 19th 2013

Kangaroo Point, Brisbane

6:32 PM

Junie Bennett was twenty years old.

It felt like only yesterday it was her tenth birthday and she was walking down the street trying to get rid of that horridly big badge Mrs David had stuck on to her shirt. How had she gotten so old so quick? She was twenty years old. Twenty years old. She couldn't rap her head around that. She did not feel twenty. She still felt like that awkwardly lanky fourteen-year-old girl who was obsessed with skateboarding and secretly pining for her best friend.

Admittedly, she still was obsessed with skateboarding. She could never give that up, even if she wanted to. Skateboarding had been drilled into her system now and there was no way it would or could ever vanish. Even though university and work took up a lot of her time,

Junie still managed to find some time at the weekend to go over to the local skate park.

"Twenty," she murmured. "Twenty."

Junie stared at her reflection in the long mirror that hung on the back of her bedroom door. Nothing much had changed. Five foot eleven. She was still awkwardly tall. Porcelain white skin. Still pale and still could not tan. Junie sighed. Birthdays, well, birthdays were not as pointless as she had originally thought.

There was something magical in celebrating the day of someone's birth. It was a great chance to show your appreciation for that person and it was a great chance for that person to appreciate what they had. At least that was what Junie tried to tell herself. It was hard to celebrate when she did not think there was anything to celebrate.

But turning twenty is something to celebrate, she told herself for probably the umpteenth time that week. It was the first time in years that she had dreaded her birthday. She had officially left her teens. Junie was not ready to be an adult.

She slumped down onto the sofa. She placed her elbows atop her thighs and buried her face in her hands. There was nothing to celebrate, there was no point in trying to convince herself otherwise. Junie swallowed, feeling the grief creeping upon as she thought of her mother.

Gone.

They always used that word when they referred to Audrey. Audrey was gone. She did not think it was possible to hate a word so much. No. Audrey was not gone. Saying she was gone implied that she would come back. Saying she was gone inferred that any minute now, any second now Audrey would waltz into the room with that air of nonchalance and melancholy about her.

Dead.

Passed away.

Deceased.

Those were the proper words to use. She preferred those words, they were clean cut, straight to the point. Unlike gone, those words did not even attempt to dress up or hide the sorrowful fact. Audrey Bennett was dead. It was a simple sentence. Easy to read. Easy to understand but harder than anything to let sink in.

It was three weeks ago, as Junie had been sat in the staff room of Lolita's taking her lunch break when Fiona had called her and told her the news. Junie had felt light-headed, Fiona's voice seeming worlds away. Something about a drug overdose. Something about Audrey having insomnia and taking too many sleeping tablets with alcohol. Something about one of the hotel staff walking in and finding Audrey's cold and motionless body lying on the couch.

Dead.

When someone died, especially someone like your mother, weren't you supposed to feel sad? Weren't you supposed to feel something? Junie did not feel anything. Just numb. Numbness everywhere.

No matter how matter times she said, saw or thought that word, that sentence, it still refused to sink in. It refused to link itself with Audrey. Dead. Audrey was dead.

"Dead," she muttered.

The funeral was scheduled in under a week. The planning had come suddenly and it was all Junie and her aunt had been doing for the past few weeks. It was stressful and unbearable but it had to be done.

A few days two days after the dreaded funeral was – or more accurately – would have been Junie and Dylan's three year anniversary. Another exasperated groan escaped her lips. It hurt to think about him. Her chest would swell with this throbbing ache that brought tears to her eyes. No wonder she had been dreading this day. It would be the first time in a decade that Dylan would miss her birthday.

Without him, it did not feel like her birthday. Nothing felt like anything without him. Junie grit her teeth and pushed away those depressive thoughts of her deceased mother and ex-boyfriend. She sucked in a deep breath and forced on a smile. If she kept smiling, then maybe, just maybe she would feel just a faint echo of happiness that used to preside within her.

She glance up at the clock. In an hour or two, Farah would be picking her up. This month had been hazardous and quite truthfully, very depressing and she needed something to lift her up. Junie, Farah and the rest of her university friends were going clubbing later that evening.

Junie was going to dress up, go dancing, get drunk and cast away her woes for just one night. If she didn't do that then, chances were invariably likely that she would end up lying on her bed crying herself to sleep.

She felt the depressive thoughts creeping back into her mind and shaking her head, she switched on the television. Junie mindlessly flicked through the channels, not really pay any attention, just changing channels for the sake of it. After a while Junie decided to watch one of those American talk shows that she really could not remember the name of but she always found quite entertaining.

The host, a cheerful woman with short blonde hair who wore a cardigan and a bright smile, was dancing around the stage, the crowd cheering and clapping along to the music. She did so for a few minutes before she twirled and skipping back onto the stage, she sat herself down on one of the two armchairs that faced the audience.

"Our second guest of the day is a singer-songwriter from Australia. He has been causing a storm in the music industry for the past couple of monthsand his debut single went number one in over fifteen countries!" she announced, "please welcome, Dylan Mercer!"

Junie felt her heart drop into her stomach. She knew she should switch off the television or at least change the channel but she was frozen, her chocolate brown eyes fixed on the large screen ahead.

As the audience cheered and wolf-whistled, Dylan walked out onto the stage. He wore this blinding smile and his ocean blue eyes were shining with excitement. The host stood up when he reached the two armchairs and once she shook his hand they both sat down.

"I'm so excited to have you on the show!" She beamed, "I'm honestly a fan of your work."

Dylan grinned, so bright and brilliant, "I'm really honoured to be on the show, Ellen."

"You've created quite buzz in the music industry, everybody's talking about you," she said, "I mean, North-lands, your debut song, is simply stunning. I think that's why it has been so successful because people of all ages can relate to the lyrics. What inspired you to write such an inspirational song?"

Junie noted how gorgeous Dylan looked. So clean cut and professional but still so Dylan. He looked a thousand times better than she had last seen him three months ago.

"I wrote that song a few months after my nineteenth birthday," he began, "I was just in this...dark place, where I really couldn't see a way out. I mean, all of my friends had to gone uni and I was working full time at a crappy call centre and I didn't know where my life was going at the point. And one night when I was feeling pretty sorry for myself, I grabbed my guitar and wrote it."

Ellen nodded along to his words. She said, "when did people start noticing you and your music?"

"I suppose it was when...uhm...the radio station that I worked at allowed me to play a song of mine," Dylan replied, "I guess people liked it because the radio station received this flood of requests for my song the next day and...and the next thing I knew people from record labels were calling me, interested in signing me and...it just went from there."

Junie remembered just how happy Dylan had been when he had first gotten that recording contract. She remembered the excitement and pride and love when she saw him perform at his first big gig in Melbourne.

She remembered how the crowds screamed and chanted his name. She remembered how hectic his schedule was. How it meant he was always away, off somewhere to perform, or promote, or do an interview.

And most of all she remembered the night they talked on the phone. She remembered the harrowing conservation that took place. The crack in her voice when she told him, they had to break up. The long and stony silence on the other end, then his heartbreaking agreement. The termination of their relationship had stung but it had been mutual. It had been necessary.

He needed to live his dream and she did not want to hold him back, because he was performing and travelling so much, they rarely go to see each other. His frequent absence had been putting an unbearable pressure on their relationship and they had to let go before the pressure permanently ripped them apart.

They promised they would still be friends. It was a bland promise. They occasionally texted and called each other just to see how the other was doing. To be honest, it hurt too much talking to him. She thought it was better if they just kept their distance for a while until they found their feet and knew what they truly wanted. Not just from each other but for themselves.

Junie watched in sombre silence as Dylan conversed with Ellen, laughing and joking and being oh so New

Zealand. Her heart squeezed and that awful ache returning in her chest. Junie blinked back the tears that were forming but as much as she tried to fight them off they came streaming down her face and for the first time in eleven years Junie found herself crying.

With tears blurring her vision, she watched as Dylan stepped onto the stage to perform. He leant into the mike, strumming the guitar and smiled straight at the camera as if he knew she was watch and sang. Not his new single but none other than The Happy Birthday Song and her heart very nearly burst out of her chest.

And the tears came in floods, everything she had bottled up since their break-up, and everything she had blocked since her mother's death. And she was sobbing, weeping uncontrollably when her aunt entered the living room.

"Junie!" Fiona gasped. She quickly rushed forward and sat down beside her. She wrapped her arms around her and pulled her into a hug, "Honey, what's wrong?"

That overwhelming wave of sorrow took over her as deep sobs wracked my body, the tears way past her control now.

"Can you call Farah and tell her I can't go out tonight?" She said, her voice thick and muffled, "I just...I don't have the energy."

Fiona nodded, and kissed her forehead, "Of course."

"I miss him," she snivelled, "I miss Audrey, I know she was a crappy mum but...she was still my mum and I...I can't believe she's gone."

Fiona hugged her tighter, kissing her forehead again, her voice smooth and comforting as she murmured, "I know, honey, I know."

Chapter 12

M onday, May 19th 2014

Kangaroo Point, Brisbane

2:03 PM

Today was Junie Bennett's twenty-first birthday and she was crying.

She didn't know why. Well, she did. But she did not know why she was crying because of it. It was silly really. She had been standing in front of the mirror in the midst of popping an earring in when it had slipped out of her grasp and onto the floor.

Junie had been crawling around on the carpeted floor in an attempt to locate the earring, when she came across a tattered looking wooden box. Curiosity getting the better of her, Junie momentarily forgot her quest for the missing earring and pulled the lid off the small box. Inside, she saw an assortment of trinkets, paper and a stack of photographs clumped together with an elastic band.

She had tentatively reached in and took out a sheet of paper. She smiled. It was one of her primary school report cards. That aching yet warm sense of nostalgia wrapped its tendrils around her heart and slowly squeezed. The teachers had painted a rather negative view of nine-year-old Junie Bennett.

Her teachers often made statements they could not back with sufficient evidence. They claimed she was too argumentative but she did not see how proving why she was right was being 'too argumentative'. They claimed she was stubborn but she did not see how refusing to apologise to Dora Seymour for pushing her when she had pushed Junie first.

They claimed she was meddlesome and Junie certainly did not see how choosing to investigate where Ms. Hornsby really went for her 'quick errands' was meddlesome. It came to be that she would venture off to the far end of the sports field to smoke. In hindsight, Junie realised that maybe she should not have taken the picture of Ms. Hornsby smoking and sneakily dropped into the principal's office.

She did feel rather guilty when Ms. Hornsby was nearly fired because of it. The teacher had asked her why she had reported her to the principal and Junie had shrugged and recited the law that specified smoking in public places was illegal. Thinking about it, maybe that was why Ms. Hornsby chose to humiliate her with that large badge on her tenth birthday.

Junie dropped the report card and rummaging through the box, she pulled out the photographs. The aching warmth intensified with every picture that she went through. Junie paused at one particular picture. It was taken two weeks before her twelfth birthday.

It showed Junie and Dylan with their arms around each other's shoulders, grinning so beamingly bright at the camera. They were sat, perched on top of the highest slopes in the skate park. That day was retained in her mind so deeply because it had been in that moment as she watched Dylan attempt to execute a three-sixty ollie and fail that she knew.

She knew that if searched for a thousand years, for a million miles in a billion universes she would never find anybody even remotely close to the sheer and complex brilliance that was Dylan Mercer.

Junie came across another picture, this one had been taken almost three years ago on their high school prom night. They were standing just outside the hotel the prom was being held. Junie was smiling at the camera, dressed in a long strapless purple dress, her red hair had been styled up into an eloquent bun with some flowers pinned in.

Dylan had his arm around her waist, his hand resting on her hip and the other hand stuffed in his trouser pocket. She remembered how handsome he looked in the black and white tuxedo. She had been staring straight at the camera, wearing a wide grin.

Dylan was not looking at the camera, instead his attention was on her. He had this look of adoration in his ocean blue eyes that stole her breath. Biting her lip, Junie placed the photographs down and continued rummaging through the box.

She picked up a clump of dark burgundy coloured rock. A small gasp left her lips. She thought she had lost it. This beautiful, jagged, odd little rock was the first birthday present she had ever received. It was the first present Dylan had given her. It was the first present anybody had ever given her. What was it that Dylan had said? What was it he had said on that hot afternoon they had first met?

"A volcanic rock," Junie murmured, "from Mount Tongariro."

Junie smiled at the memory.

It was times like this that Junie missed Dylan more than anything. She missed his infectious grin and that soft laugh, she missed the way his face would light up every time he mastered a new chord or learnt a new skateboarding trick. She missed the way he was able to make her gloomy mood vanish with just one flash of that sunshine smile.

And that was when Junie had started to cry. The bittersweet and aching warmth filling her chest had gotten too much and now she was crying. Before she went into a sobbing frenzy, Junie quickly wiped the tears away with the sleeve of her sweater. As she snivelled, she placed the volcanic rock and the other items she had taken out back into the box. She settled the lid back on and slid the box underneath her bed, where she had found it.

Junie found her thoughts slipping to that dismal day of Audrey's funeral. Junie had not cried that day. She assumed she would but had not. Although Isaiah had cried for three days straight after the funeral. All she did, all she could do was stare blankly ahead, Fiona's eulogy falling on deaf ears. Junie shook her head, willing those thoughts to leave her mind.

It was stupid really. Stupid and pointless to cry over the past. What was the point of mourning the past when the future held so much promise? It was her twenty-first birthday and she found herself hoping it would be a good one. Dylan would not be able to make it, since he had a gig in Berlin and two television interviews after. It could still be a good birthday even if he could not be present.

Junie had to look on the bright side. In the evening, she would be going to the best restaurant in Queensland for her birthday dinner and in two days, she would be going to Sydney for a weeklong vacation. It was going to be a week of clubbing, sunbathing, surfing and joking around with her friends. Farah had come over yesterday and helped Junie finish packing for their vacation. For the first time in a long while, Junie was actually looking forward to something.

She picked up the earring she had dropped and once she put it on, she walked towards her door. She had just grasped the handle when she heard it. A melody, sweet and soft, had drifted into the room and encircled her in its familiar warmth. She froze, her entire body tensing when a voice, a memorable voice accompanied the saccharine music.

"Hey you, I heard it's your birthday,
And I just wanted to say,
I'm so glad it's your birthday,
And I just wanted to say.
I'm so glad it's your birthday."

Junie's head whipped back and forth as she desperately tried to find the source of the music. Junie quickly walked forward and pushing the window open, she leaned out. And her heart froze. There, standing in her back garden, merrily playing a guitar and wearing this sunny smile was Dylan Mercer.

"I'll make your loneliness fade away,

Just hold my hand, and everything will be okay.

As long as you have me,

I swear you will never feel like yesterday".

Dylan's once mid-length hair that had swooped across his forehead in messy waves was longer there. It was much shorter now with a graceful and classic quiff like James Dean. He was no longer that short and skinny boy she had met eleven years ago.

He here was, a fully grown twenty-one-year-old musician, a rather famous musician and she could not remember him look more handsome. The sight of him ultimately caused her heartstrings to tug and quiver. Something no one else except him had ever achieved to do. She momentarily wondered if she was dreaming.

"Hey you, I heard it's your birthday,

And I just wanted to say,

I'm so glad it's your birthday,

And I just wanted to say.

I'm so glad it's your birthday."

And as she stood there, leaning out of her bedroom window, watching Dylan sing in absolute stunned silence, Junie felt herself being transported back. Back to her sixteenth birthday, to that late evening in his garden.

Gazing up at him with so much adoration, with the soft grass beneath her feet, the cool breeze swimming around her and the glowing red sky above.

"And I am here to say,

To scream at the top of my lungs,

So the whole world can hear me now,

Happy birthday to you"

His voice, sweeter than honey and stronger than titanium echoed throughout the garden. And she felt light-headed and dazed. As he sung the last note, their eyes locked and silence reigned as they stared at each other.

"New Zealand?" Junie whispered, not quite believing her eyes.

He grinned that brilliant sunshine smile that she hadn't seen in so long. "Hi, Junebug."

"I...I...You..."

Without a moment's hesitation, Junie pushed herself from the window and ran out of her bedroom. With her heart beating deafeningly loud in her chest, she darted down the hallway, down the stairs, past the living room where six-year-old Isaiah was playing on his Xbox, past the kitchen where Fiona was preparing lunch and straight into the back garden.

Junie came to an abrupt halt, stopping by the door. Her breathing was ragged, not from the running but from the rush of seeing him again. He was really here. She was not dreaming. Dylan was here. They stood several metres apart, Junie was barefoot and dressed in a vest top and shorts, staring disbelievingly at her childhood best friend.

Dylan was dressed like he had come from an elegant party, dressed in a black and white suit that made him look unfairly handsome, looking nervously at her as he fiddled with the strings of his guitar. If she moved even an inch, she was scared he would disappear.

"W-what are you doing here?" She stammered, taking a tentative step forward, "I thought you had a gig in Berlin?"

"I...I cancelled it," he said softly, "I needed to see you."

"Right..." She said because that was the only thing she could manage. She gestured to his formal attire, "Where did you just come from?"

"Uhm, the Australian movie premiere for X-Men: Days of Future Past," he answered, still looking adorably shy. "It was awesome, we should go see it sometime...together, I mean...if-if you want to..."

She had seen him in interviews, she had seen how eloquent and confident and charming he was, he had countless women head over heels in love with. But with her, he acted like a love-struck teenager and she did not know what to make of it, of him. She ignored the way her stomach knotted at his offer and said, "What are you doing here?"

His gaze flitted to the floor and then back up to meet her eyes. "I wanted to see you," he replied, "I've only seen you four times in the past year and I...I miss you."

Her heart quickened and she stepped forward, "Dylan...Dylan, I–"

"I'm sorry I missed your birthday," he interrupted, "I'm so sorry I wasn't there for you when your mum died, it's just...everything happened so quick y'know? One day I'm sat in my boxers eating from a can of soup and the next thing I know I'm performing on stage in front of six thousand people," he said in a heated rush, "Don't get me wrong, I love singing and music but...it didn't really feel like music without you. Nothing felt like anything without you."

His eyes were that familiar piercing ocean blue that for as long as she could remember would always make her melt. And that was he was doing right then, the same thing he always did, ensnaring her in his blue eyes.

"Dylan."

"I just...I can't really...how do I explain....?" he stammered, "I feel...I feel like I'm the moon and you're the sun."

Junie stared at him, "What's that supposed to mean?"

"I can't shine without you."

She laughed, feeling elation and warmth fill her chest, "You're so cheesy."

He blushed and damn her if it wasn't the most endearing sight on earth. "Shut up, you love it."

There were so many things she wanted to say to him in that moment. All the words she had never said throughout the years just bubbling inside of her and waiting to be released but they jammed in her throat and all she could do was just stare feebly at him.

Junie let out a small sigh and tilting her head, she looked up at the cloudless afternoon sky. And for a moment, she felt like she was ten and walking home with that badge stuck to her top. She gasped when she felt the sudden collision of Dylan's body against hers as he wrapped his arms around her and pulled her into a tight hug.

He buried his head in the nook between her neck and shoulder and hugged her tighter. Junie closed her eyes and letting her chin fall on his shoulders, she breathed him in. And he smelt like home. Like everything she wanted and everything she could possibly need. They stayed like that for a while, standing in the middle of the back garden, tightly holding onto one another.

Dylan slowly lifted his head and she felt heat pool into her stomach as his soft lips grazed the shell of ear. "What do you say, Junebug?"

"To what?"

"You and me," he whispered, "until the end of time."

A smile pulled at her lips, the answer slipping out of her mouth effortlessly, "Sounds good."

She felt his smile against the skin of her bare shoulder, the sensation of his lips pressing into her skin made her heart drum hard. His hands slowly coasted her back, the other had moved to rest on her hip. He pulled back to look at her, a warm smile shaped his lips as he gazed at her. And she felt as if she was caught in the direct heat of the sun. It made her cheeks turn red as heat beat through her.

"You know," he began gently, "You know I love you right?"

She was grinning now, "I know, I know, I love you too Dyl."

He mirrored her elated grin, staring gleefully at her for a long moment. He kissed her then, and if she wasn't so happy she would cry at finally, finally, after two years having his lips on hers. It was soft and lingering and warm enough to send her heart into a frenzy.

"Happy birthday, Junie," he said when they separated.

She had missed him. Missed them. Missed this so much she felt as if she couldn't breathe for a moment. She dropped her head on his chest, laughing because she felt almost drunk with happiness.

Her eyes slid shut as she swallowed and smiled, "Thanks New Zealand."

Epilogue

T uesday, May 20th 2025

Chichester, England

1:10 PM

The church doors swing open, the afternoon light showers the guests in its warmth as they all stand.

And here comes the bride. Her dress, white and pristine, flows down the length of her body. The very epicentre of the wedding, looking as graceful and beautiful as the sun. Her face is hidden behind the veil but a smile can be seen as her eyes lock with the groom.

As the bride takes her place at the altar, her father lightly kisses her hand and goes to sit down. She passes her colourful bouquet of roses to her maid of honour and taking a deep breath, she turns to face the groom. His smile is infectious and she can't help but smile back. The guests sit themselves down as the priest clears his throat and calls for attention.

"Ladies and gentlemen, family and friends," the priest begins, smiling benevolently, "we are gathered here today to witness and celebrate the joining of Robert Angeles and Farah Finley. With love and commitment, they have decided to live their lives together as husband and wife."

Junie cannot help smiling either as she watches her best friend wed the man of her dreams. The planning and preparation for the wedding has been absolute mayhem. When she met up with Farah eight months ago, she expected their standard coffee date and catch up about their lives, what she did not expect was Farah to announce Bobby proposed and that she wanted Junie to be the maid of honour.

It took four stressful months to find the perfect wedding dress and it was worth it because Farah looks stunning. Her dress, however, is a little tight and but she did not want to bring up the matter on the day of wedding as Farah was already stressed and freaking out about all the things that could wrong.

The bible readings and the vows pass by in a saccharine blur and as they exchange rings and make promises to love each other until their deaths, Junie is reminded of her own wedding. Of seven years ago in a small church in Brisbane. Of the rush that came with being pronounced man and wife and their first dance underneath the stars.

She steals a glance at her husband. Dylan is sat in the second row, looking exceptionally handsome in his tuxedo. His eyes suddenly meet hers, and in the twenty-two years they have known each other and in the seven years they have been married, his piercing blue eyes never fail to make her heart flutter. His mouth widens into a bright grin and he gives her a thumbs up. Junie smiles at him and returns her attention to the bride and groom, just in time to see them kiss. The entire church breaks into applause and a few wolf whistles.

7:34 PM

Junie Mercer watches from her seat as Farah and Bobby take to their first dance as husband and wife. She smiles to herself. Last night, during her hen night, Farah revealed she's three weeks pregnant. Bobby's a great man and she imagines the two of them are going to fantastic parents.

"Junebug."

She looks up at the sound of her nickname. Dylan's stood before her, holding a glass filled to the brim with champagne and another with orange juice as he smiles warmly. He passes her a drink and sits himself down on the seat next to her.

Of course, nobody can quite believe that Dylan Mercer, the internationally famous singer-songwriter, is at the wedding. It's a good thing most of the people are close friends of theirs. For probably the umpteenth time that day, she thinks that he looks very handsome in his suit, she's seen many of the women stealing glances at him and she feels sense of triumph every time they frown as they catch the gold wedding band around his finger. He's going to be performing later, singing some of his best hits and a special number he wrote just for Bobby and Farah.

"So," he says as he takes a sip of the champagne, "How does it feel?"

"How does what feel?"

"To finally be a professor," he says and clears his throat, leaning in towards her and he smells like always does. He smells like home. He talks in a low husky tone that causes something in chest to spread with warm, "Professor Juniper Mercer of Astrophysics at Cambridge University."

Junie swallows. He makes it sound a million times sexier than it actually is. It was last week when she finished her black hole physics lecture for second-year students that she got the call to visit the dean of the university's office. And after nine years, dozens of research papers, experiments and expeditions she was finally granted the professorship she's been wanting since she was fourteen.

The dean said it was her paper on the possibility of warp-speed travel in space that gained her the tenure. Her calculations and experiments on the matter are already being tested and the results are mixed but if they keep refining it, it will no doubt be a success. At this rate, there is a chance her equations and research can be used for future expeditions into space.

"It has a nice ring don't you think, Professor Mercer?" Dylan grins at her. "I have no doubt they'll put you on the team for the manned space expedition to Mars. You're one of the best astrophysicists in the world, you are going to get it. And just you watch Junie, when we go to Mars, you are going to be the lead scientists behind it all and you're name is going down in the history books."

She laughs at her husband. He has always been a dreamer. She lifts her hands and lightly caresses his cheek, enjoying the rough feel of his stubble. Time has been more than kind to him, he seems to be getting more handsome with each passing year. She smiles, "How can you possibly know that?"

"Because you've been my best friend since were ten and I know just how brilliant you are," he answers with such ease, she forgets how to breathe for a few moments.

He flashes her a cheeky grin and glances over at Bobby and Farah dancing to the slow music. They seem so lost in each other; she sees the nostalgic smile on his lips and knows he's thinking of their wedding. Her hand subconsciously goes to play with her wedding ring, turning it around her finger, the same nostalgic smile on her face.

"You know," he says in a gentle voice as he glances at her, "You're a pretty good wife."

She laughs, ignoring the way heart picks up at that. "Pretty good? I'm the best damn wife you'll ever have."

"Can't say I disagree," he says.

He leans forward, gaze locked on her lips and kisses her. And after all this time, he still kisses like she's fragile glass and his kisses are still sweet, if not sweeter and leave her wanting more. She can feel him smiling. The feel of his silky hair as she runs her fingers through it, the taste of his mouth and the smell of his cologne fills her senses, dulling the surrounding world out.

When they pull apart, Junie giggles like she's seventeen and falling in love for the first time. Dylan presses a quick kiss to her cheek and leans back in his chair.

Junie glances longily at his champagne.

He must notice because he laughs and says, "Sorry, honey but you know can't have alcohol."

Her hand goes to rest on her stomach, she smiles, she can definely feel the bump now. Junie found out she was pregnant with twins in January, and it was only last week, after months of debate that they were finally told the gender.

Even now she can hardly believe it. Twins are going to be a handful, especially boys but she doesn't mind. She feels as if she can do anything with Dylan by her side.

"I know," she says, smiling wider.

"I was thinking," he says, "about the names for the boys, I know we agreed on Max for the first twin, how about Lennon for the second?"

"Lennon, as in John Lennon or as in your dad?" she asks.

He, at least, has the decency to look a little sheepish as he nods. He rubs the back of his neck, "Both, really. John Lennon was the whole reason I even got into music and my dad is the best guy ever so,it would mean a lot to me, Junebug."

He looks so nervous and excited, like he's on the brink of greatness. She has the strong urge to kiss him until the world stop turning. Her smile widens into a grin. God, she loves him so much.

"Lennon," she repeats, testing the feel of it in her mouth. Junie nods, "yeah, Lennon. Max and Lennon Mercer. I like it."

The way he smiles and the way blue eyes explode with light almost knocks the air from her lungs. He looks like a child on Christmas.

"Really?" he gasps and when she nods, he cups her face and pulls her into a kiss that has her toes curling and heart drumming in her chest.

"There are children present," Someone says, causing them to pull apart. They glance up to find Isaiah sat on the other side of the circular table. He wears a feigned look of disgust as he takes long gulps of his bottled drink. "Jesus, you're thirty-two years old. You can't be making out like you're teenagers."

Junie tries hard not to wince. Yesterday was her birthday and she doesn't think it's an old age, but her brother makes her sound and feel rather ancient.

She notices the beer in his hand and quickly takes it from him.

"Hey!" he shouts.

"Zee, what the hell, this is alcohol," she frowns, "How many times? You're not allowed beer."

"I'm turning eighteen next month!"

"Yeah, next month," she says, "until then, no beer. Aunt Fiona let you get away with a lot things but not with me, there are rules and you are going to abide them."

At seventeen, Isaiah has grown into quite the heart-throb. She's seen the way all the girls at his school and outside immediately zero in on him and turn into blushing idiots whenever he looks their way. He loves the attention.

"Aren't sisters supposed to be fun?" He asks with a huff, "I miss Fiona. I miss Australia. I wanna go back."

"I don't care," she says, "Fiona sent you to live with us because you were being an arse and she needs some space from you. Fiona's married with two step-children and she doesn't need you wreaking havoc and causing her more stress. You're stuck in England with us, so deal with it."

"Go flirt with some girls," Dylan says, "There are plenty here that are your age."

Isaiah rolls his eyes, "They're boring, I mean at least half of them have boyfriends, like what the hell is that about?"

She sometimes finds herself missing the bright sun and the salty smell of Brisbane. They have been living in England for a little over four years now and she's glad they made the leap to move here.

They have a nice house near Cambridge that has a picturesque view of the surrounding countryside, it's not far from the university, where she teaches and carries out most of her research. She likes it because the crime is low, the air is fresh, the people are kind and the town is lively and has plenty to go see and do. The perfect place to raise their children.

"Actually," she looks around the large hall, frowning slightly, "Where is Astrid?"

It's then that she spots the familiar head of fiery red hair a few feet away. She's laughing as she talks to Farah's nephew, the five-year-old ring bearer with a messy head of blonde hair and a shy smile. Astrid looks absolutely adorable in that puffy white dress and the roses in her hair adds volumes to her sheer cuteness.

She leans forward and whispers something in the boy's ear and they both burst into a giggling fit. She glances over at them and taking the boy's hand in hers, Astrid walks over to them. Junie nudges Dylan's shoulder as the two children head in their direction.

"Mum, Dad," Astrid greets when she reaches their table, "This is Vince, he's my new friend!"

She's staring up at them with these big blue eyes and a bright grin. Astrid may have Junie's fiery hair but she has Dylan's eyes, a bright ocean blue and the freckles he had when they were kids, they smatter her nose and plump cheeks.

Well, Junie thinks, she's only four but Junie knows her daughter is going to be an absolute heartbreaker when she's older. Vince looks rather nervous, smiling at them with the same watery green eyes that all members of the Finley family possess.

"Uhm, hi," he says. "C-can I have...have this dance with 'Trid?"

Junie, Dylan and Isaiah share amused looks and glance back at the pair of children. Dylan smiles, "You don't need to ask us, buddy. Go on, have fun!"

Astrid and Vince simultaneously break out into grins. Astrid tugs at the little boy's hand, pulling him towards the dance floor, "Come on V," she says, "Let's go."

Junie watches their daughter and her new friend run to the dance floor.

"Right," Isaiah says as he runs his hand through his short blonde hair and pushing his chair back, he stands up, "If you'll excuse me, there's a certain brunette by the bar who I've been meaning to chat to."

His chocolate brown eyes are bright as he gives them his trademark grin and walks off. Junie turns to her husband and sees him stand up too. He reaches his hand out to her, the most charming smile on his lips, "Would you care to dance, Junebug?"

"Of course, New Zealand," she laughs as she takes his hand.